BEACH BIRDS

Beach Birds

SEVERO SARDUY

Translated from the Spanish
by Suzanne Jill Levine & Carol Maier

Fn Bella,

7/7

Love,
Jiee

OTIS BOOKS / SEISMICITY EDITIONS
The Graduate Writing Program
Otis College of Art and Design
LOS ANGELES ● 2007

Published originally as *Pájaros de la playa*
   (Barcelona: Tusquets Editores, S.A., 1993)
English translation ©2007, Suzanne Jill Levine and Carol Maier

Book design and typesetting: Yuko Sawamoto

ISBN: 978–09755 9 24–8–9

OTIS BOOKS / SEISMICITY EDITIONS
The Graduate Writing Program
Otis College of Art and Design
9045 Lincoln Boulevard
Los Angeles, CA 90045

www.otis.edu
www.gw.otis.edu
seismicity@otis.edu

◯◯➤ TABLE OF CONTENTS

1

BEACH BIRDS

The powerful feet of the runners left tracks momentarily on the reddish sand. The runners sped by, concentrating on their exercise as if thinking about each muscle they tightened, absorbed in their daily offering to health. Exaggerated outlines, their taut, almost metallic bodies glistened, varnished with sweat; wet locks of hair stuck to their skulls.

They went off into the distance, without glancing for a moment at the few bathers basking in the sun or recovering from their drunken staggering of the night before by breathing the coastal air.

Tall palms topped with dark green leafy tufts: the only verticals in sight.

Toward the interior of the island, beyond the sand, a mound of rocks stretched for several kilometers, frequented only by intolerant nudists and red-crested chameleons.

The nudists stood on the highest rocks, raising their tensed arms until their hands touched above their heads, inhaling the pure air, the live air of the shore; then they began to lower them little by little, expelling the same air now contaminated by the insides of their opaque pulmonary bodies. They were beach birds just before embarking on their first flight, rehearsing their fragile wings, ready to tackle the oceanic whirlwinds.

An angry throb pulsed in the blood-red throats of the chameleons as they threatened the invaders' feet, perhaps thinking they were still the dinosaurs they had been in a distant yesterday.

The landscape, seen from an eventual airplane, would be the simple juxtaposition of three bands: transparent, mobile blue, reddish beige, rumpled ochre.

Night was falling. In the middle of the island, a well-lit highway marked the axis of the island's symmetry. Excessively slow aluminum trucks traversed the highway as if in a dream, or as if their drivers were intoxicated and afraid of being fined. They were asking precisely for that by moving at such a lethargic pace.

At the nearby airport, when you go in the opposite direction from the landing strips, planes, every light blazing, turn into ships cautiously descending, as though afraid to touch down, almost stationary.

On the rocky walls, the gregarious nudists had left an inscription of their binges and other bouts: a sign engraved with flint – double salamander, maybe a bird – repeated without variation. Years ago, the congregation had been multitudinous and mobile.

Today it was nothing. Aged and anemic. The young bucks' streaking by was a mere show of reverence to their parents' ecological rhetoric, a sign of their abomination for swimming trunks – they disparaged the covered bathers, abusively calling them "textiles" – or for any inactivity.

The surviving naturists plunged between rocks, as if descending steps carved in the stone. Creeping like worms spewed by the sea and now seeking to escape the voracity of preying birds, they clambered between the crags in order to camouflage their presence, to flee what they most hated: the gaze of the other.

They lived lying down. Only one stood – simulating his breathing exercises –, the one responsible for scrutinizing the coast, for keeping an eye on each group and guarding the rites of nudity.

They dwelled where the soil was clayish; the most vehement of them buried themselves in consecutive tunnels: a labyrinth with no visible design, no plan, which apparently obeyed only their drive to dig.

But what, seen at ground level, evoked a confusion of clumsy tunnels went on to reveal, seen from above – from a possible airplane –, its meticulous structure: an outrageous sign, identical to the one repeated across the rocks. An entire world of hiding places and catacombs.

Or, simply, the remains of some exaggerated summertime amusement.

Who was about to show up among the crags, among the chameleons, iguanas, jumping lizards and other animals – all swift and shining as lightning flashes? Who but a lively, tail-wagging, iridescent, leathery, scaly island saurian brimming with poison and poison's immaterial equivalent: science?

Herb therapy has brought him to this jungle island, an exact reflection of the other island in the ocean's mercury. He's meditating now, remembering a melancholy, dark green royal palm.

Like the reptiles among the rocks, sects proliferate here in search of a return to the Edenic life of our early purity – free from all technical perversions. There are also some sects that build secret airports under the sea, waiting for ships.

Where better than here for the saurian to introduce his crafty phytogenic pharmacopoeia?

He walked around naked. And when he wasn't naked, he dressed in white from head to toe. Apparently that's best.

2

THE PENTAGON

Beyond the highway are the others, the ones whom energy has abandoned.

They are housed in the center garden, in a vast mansion with Moorish walls that still stand solid: sloping arches and tiled doorway lintels; a hypothetical Koran in a little turret scatters its calligraphies.

Along one of the five corridors with whitewashed walls and white mosaic floors leading to the garden, an unkempt blonde girl approaches; she seems to be a sleepwalker, disheveled and bald as she gets closer. She wears thick glasses and a frayed red housecoat. She looks very busy concentrating on some idea or on a distant memory she's trying in vain to revive. On her left arm, she neglectfully wears the complex rolling apparatus of her own transfusion, also what appear to be printed sheets of paper, as if dragging a toy hoop or an old rag doll; indolent, her head in the clouds.

The center garden is, of course, a pentagon; glass isosceles triangles form the structure of the roof; the assemblage is golden.

Through the triangles you can make out a cirrhotic sky; above the highway, the stripes of a rainbow are clearly outlined. One end rests on the palms and the distant mountains, the other on the towers of a church in ruins. It gradually vanishes toward the sea.

Birds passed high overhead, seeking rocks along the coast to build their nests, as if they'd known that route for millennia. Intrigued by the glass polyhedron, some of them circled around it or perched on the top, inspecting those inside; then they flew off cawing and squawking.

They were not old, those emaciated, sallow, toothless men with trembling hands and dry eyes. Seated on the iron benches against the pentagon, wrapped in loose sport shirts, were young men struck suddenly by the malady, withered prematurely by their failing strength.

All of them gazed upward, toward the glass panes, as if they were birdwatchers waiting for the flight of a rare species; or perhaps awaiting nightfall so that they could return along the long corridors to their cells and sink once again into the dream whence they could never completely break free.

The disheveled girl with the transfusion came to join the group.

"Waiting for birds?"

"They already passed," answered the frail man on the bench with a smile that outlined the tiny wrinkles in the corners of his eyes and around his lips.

"A sand storm?"

"No: the light is healing. Today we can see all of its seven colors. The sky is brimming with the same strength that we've come to lack."

Another old man came to add to the conversation, as if the lack of strength excused the lack of any social protocol. He was probably about thirty, but had no hair left. A joking or resigned expression was fixed on his face in which his wide-open yellow eyes sparkled, vigilant and owl-like: dry opals.

"The light is healing, but not for me. My spirit, no longer inhabiting my body, has left me. What now eats, sleeps, speaks and defecates amidst the others is only a simulation. The sun is encouraging, it's true, but something in your skin has to catch it, and that's precisely what disappears with the malady. Here

I am, beneath the rosy daylight, but now it's all posthumous. I escaped from physical suffering."

"How?" inquired the girl with the transfusion.

"Absenting myself from my body. Abandoning it like a bundle of foul smelling clothes, something that's not only useless but annoying, unbearable. Leaving the body to those who scrutinize its disincarnation."

The girl with the transfusion listened, now gripping rather than transporting her apparatus, as if she were afraid she'd lose her balance and fall.

They separated at dusk. A strong wind cleared the sky.

That night you could see all the stars.

The old men were also beach birds.

Years ago, some of them ran mile after mile over the sand. They were eurhythmic athletes, proud as archers, discus or javelin throwers embraced by the strong sun of the archipelago.

Now, afflicted with the malady, incapable of soaring into the sky, they spend the days remembering feats of the past. Even so, their bodies retain some of yesterday's majesty – the sharpness of their gaze, a pit-trap lying in wait, turned toward the top of the dome, as if in hopes of a heavenly diurnal sign.

"Life will return."

"Life will return."

"Yes, but which one?"

"The other one. Death is like a change of clothes. I have felt the movement of my drowned body trying to be reborn, to breathe clear air. I even sense the place: on another island."

They lifted their arms with effort. The day's major plan was formulated:

"We'll walk to the linden trees."

A sudden storm pounded the colonial mansion. Hail stones hit with such force that they shattered the glass panes of the dome. A wind capable of driving people mad blew cold like a hurricane.

A dying heron, ever on the lookout for a trickle of water, landed on the window of the bewildered blonde. The bird's feathers were matted, its pupils glassy; it looked as if it had plunged into some sticky, sickening, lethal substance. Opening its beak to vomit green drivel, the bird was wracked by the spasms of a final seizure. It unfolded its wings, straightened its iridescent neck, spread the membranes of its feet, as if about to swim. Then it became immobile. The gusts moved its feathers lightly: a wet fan.

The girl with the transfusion freed herself from her apparatus as best she could and ran from the room screaming: a cotton trail of sheets stained with iodine and blood.

The old men had grouped together in the hallway. Lightning-struck and stiff, birds fell on the glass triangles, the towers, and the roofs.

"They suffer too, from the malady," one of the ancients assured them wisely. He was probably about twenty and his face was covered with blotches.

"Like cats," he added. "Their corpses stink up the outlying slums. Mangy buzzards come to the feast. They leave immaculate skeletons, scaffolds of bone – toys for child beggars, or for the healthy cats in the neighborhood."

Another of the old men stopped short in his wheelchair. Its tires squeaked against the linoleum on the floor, which had just been disinfected by a compulsive cleaning woman. Another, sharper squeal followed the first; it was his voice, the sharp, tense thread of his raspy voice imprisoned in a guttural gasp.

His huge, sparkling new shoes seemed to get in his way. The perfectly intact soles and the precisely tied laces bothered him. He turned his body. Lifted his head. When he raised his right hand, his index finger trembled:

"Let others resign themselves; not me. Despite my frail frame I have one freedom left: to rise up against divine disorder, against the simulacrum of universal harmony. God watches indifferently as men and birds fall, struck down by lightning.

The victims are chosen at random, as in a galaxy the star that will be consumed."

His thin voice sounded in the corridor, as if it came from a tin horn.

The other old men and the girl with the transfusion lowered their eyes as if they were frightened by such blasphemy or moved by the speech of a madman.

"We're the aborted dream of a minor demiurge," he continued, "one who's very nice and well-intended but also quite clumsy. Almost everything turned out ass-backwards for him, or uselessly complicated, or vaguely approximate, or wretched...."

The thump of a bird on the roof tiles ended his diatribe. The girl with the transfusion crossed her arms. She was trembling.

Suddenly, in the abrupt way it had begun, the storm ended. The old men, who were speaking very loudly in order to counter the din or the rain, lowered their voices and began to open the windows so they could breathe the new air, the cool freshness rising from the soaked earth.

The wind had swept away the last leaves, which were accumulating all along the garden in small yellow and purple piles against the walls of the mansion. Among the piles, like sculptures of melted wax in which the original forms are barely recognizable, lay dead birds that seemed like stained rags abandoned to the elements: the dregs of the hurricane.

They walked about gathering them one at a time with excessive, rather exasperating care. They had already prepared large transparent plastic bags which they carried hung over their arms as if they were about to go shopping. This is how the birds were wrapped for their final journey.

No one had the strength to climb up to the roof – they could barely take the stairs, which were not very steep, to the Arabian tower – to gather the birds. They would let them rot...the buzzards would handle the cleanup.

They piled the birds behind the kitchen.
Fire.

The next day – they were so depleted by their funereal efforts that no one had the strength to get up.

They focused on one goal: the image of themselves dressed, freshly washed, shaved, healthy and perfumed, writing, reading, alert and jubilant beneath the morning sun. They tried to achieve that image...

First: lower your right leg until it touches the floor. Then straighten up little by little, supporting yourself with the left hand. Careful with your vertebrae. Support yourself on the edge of the bed with the right hand. Sit up. Reach for a sock. Put it on. One step toward the ideal image, which is, after all, quite attainable.

Some of them successfully followed the model they had outlined, reaching that brief moment of bliss. They displayed their shod feet, their clean socks and even a tie, like trophies, regalia won in some heroic conquest. They were exhilarated, almost intoxicated by the honor of being clean, distanced from the discreet, though still nauseating smell of their illness, far away from the morbid space of contaminated medicinal air: a fleeting, fictitious, precarious freedom, like all the rest. But, for an instant, real.

Others abandoned the project after a few fumbling gestures. It was too much. Too much for today. And they went back to bed, exhausted.

Tomorrow is another day.

3

HARPER'S BAZAAR

Immortelle had settled into the colonial mansion as if it were a deluxe hotel. She had shipped her furniture and brought her entire panoply of cosmetics – and her collection of Harper's Bazaar – for a benign retreat.

In a large wrinkled suitcase, covered with locks and little keys like the trunk of cautious drug dealers, she brought garments so diverse that they seemed to come from different centuries: salmon-colored gloves with visible stitches, feathered hats with varnished cherries – peacock feathers were either lucky or unlucky, according to the magic in vogue –, and even high-heeled boots like those worn by Uzbekistan peasants to dance in a *kolkhoz*. In the false bottom of the trunk she hid a collection of color photographs retouched by hand: garish cadmium mustard yellow plastered the hair of a military officer; the sky in the background, cerulean blue, was uniform and harsh.

Immortelle was a true crone, not a prematurely aged young woman on whose face the malady had scrawled its senescent ravages. She had straight hair, colored carrot and henna; her perfectly arched eyebrows were penciled shiny black, her eyelids silver-plated, her lips, Art Deco.

Under her left eye she sometimes dotted a beauty mark. She had decided to live with the men who considered themselves plague-ridden, "because they were young, and there's nothing worse than loneliness."

She was accompanied nonetheless by a wisp of a cat miniaturized by genetic manipulation – "Classic cats take up too much space" – who was as gluttonous and sedentary as an Antarctic seal, and even purred in his sleep.

Immortelle, like all the other inmates, and despite her good demeanor, was subjected to the regular examinations that denounced or ruled out the presence of the malady. The tortuous tangles woven by the plague – if indeed there were any – were unidentifiable: maybe it was all the result of those furious demons who thirst for animal lymph and populate the astral sphere. Or else the effect of iridescent orangutans, more mischievous and manly than men, whose morbid blood clotted, right after the hunt and before the summer battles, the skin of the warriors of certain tribes. Their tattoos provide a pattern for their scars. The infected remain invisible, protected by their bloodied ochre arabesque ornaments, but contaminated from head to toe by the malady. With equal ease they win and die.

For Immortelle, the days and names mattered little. She would note the rhythm of the seasons and fall back to sleep. Beyond her moisturizing creams, extracts and tinctures, which she kept in glazed asymmetrical bottles, as if they were poisons, everything about the hurried though regular footsteps of the nurses was unreal.

She would get up at dawn and rush to the three-mirrored Japanese vanity where she lamented the stigmas on her forehead and her profile. Diligently applying her cosmetics, she conspired against them.

Thus engaged, she was surprised by the robust gypsies of the paramedic team, an obsequious pair making their rounds with fried donuts and hot chocolate.

When her blood sample was taken – she slumped like a spongy doll in her rococo armchair – the aide then rested the filled tube among the make-up bottles.

Absent-mindedly.

At night, she sometimes recovered a sense of time, time folding and unfolding like a paper house.

The first thing she would do then was to dress. Gold-braided gowns, turbans of concentric sequins staring like eyes, silk saris. She paraded them as if in a fashion show, imperceptible by dint of repetition, amid orthopedic apparatuses, stethoscopes, lavage tubes and dirty syringes deposited for the moment in her room.

When they still had the strength to move about, or could do so on crutches, the anemic men in striped pajamas attended her shows and reverently admired her fashions, with the respect imposed by an inaugural ceremony or a funeral.

At the same time that she endorsed her outfits and costume jewelry, Immortelle related, in flowery speech, the history – every day it was different – of her acquisitions: imperial gifts, robberies, flea markets, thrift shops, or – supreme narcissism – simply her own creations.

Thus the days passed, with reminiscences, gauze bandages and gemstones.

Until one morning in front of the mirror a malaise assaulted her, a sensation she thought she had left behind forever by moving to the colonial mansion: she felt superfluous.

Imitating his mistress, the miniature cat stopped washing himself. His nose turned cold and dry. He licked Immortelle's hands at length and disappeared out the window.

Immortelle abandoned fashion shows and stories. She sold her splendid garments to the highest bidder. She declared herself evicted, abandoned, postponed and poised to disappear. She was overcome by sudden fainting spells, or she pretended. To everything she replied: "What do I care?"

Thus three months passed, according to the convoluted calculation of human time; for her, this meant only distorted or fading images of her life incoherently tumbling one after the other, as if seen at the same time from different angles, or tallied by a madman, devoid of real substance.

Not clinging to anything or anyone, as if calmly descending a shady hill, near the silent shore where she was about to surrender, to let herself die.

When he arrived.

4

THE MAN WHO WAS LIKE A HORSE

Liberated from her apparatus, the gal with the transfusion ran through the corridors in a sailor suit – all the rage in children's wear in the fifties. Now, won over by neighborly love, she was pushing the wheelchair of the guy who spoke in a pitched voice, like an Indian. At siesta time, she led him under a cluster of linden trees, not far from the big house. The shade of the leaves calms the nerves.

Sometimes, to get a game going, as "El Aleijadinho" spoke about the stars, the sailor girl let him roll down the hill, down the slopes connected by wood rails rather than steps, until the chair stopped on its own. Twangy squeaks: insults and curses.

One sleepless dawn – pelicans passed all night long – the sailor girl went into Immortelle's room, whose inhabitant, at this hour, was still lulled by a hangover from the sleeping pill.

"News," she uttered poker-faced. She too had become an apparatus, one that mechanically reproduced the voice.

"From the world of fashion?" Immortelle, between two waters, inquired.

"No. A new vampire."

They had baptized thus the young interns or cautious male nurses who collected for analysis the dubious blood of the inmates.

"What's he like?" questioned Immortelle, emerging from her stupor in the wink of an eye.

"Big and strong. With thick hair and a horse face. When he comes into a place he seems to sniff the air, as if afraid. He walks with big strides. He shows his gums when he smiles. I don't know his name."

Two days later, cautiously pushing open the door, the man who was like a horse appeared early in the morning. Immortelle, bouncy and energetic, recognized him immediately. The white coat barely covered his equine corpulence. In a little three-leveled cart, like the dessert carts in pretentious restaurants, the arsenal of blood samples followed him, jingling and sinister.

"Good morning. I am..."

"I already know."

"How?"

"A premonition."

"May I?"

"At your service."

Immortelle dropped into her armchair – the slightest effort left her breathless – as if tumbling upon a bed of fresh leaves at the edge of a stream after a summer race. She offered him her right arm with her fist already closed, without the least apprehension. She imagined it all came down to a glass sphere in the purplish red of a stained glass window, with a plump and greedy leech poised to suck. It reassured her to date the medical protocol back to its origins, as if in those sulphurous centuries of exorcism and garlic, everything had been painless, sedating and efficient.

She felt nothing. Except – when he untied the tourniquet and ordered her to open her hand – his hands brushing between her legs, the rough cloth of his pants.

"The best thing," she said to him calmly, "is to eliminate the putrifying fluids of the body and extract the small calcinated stones from the brain."

He replied with a belly laugh that sounded, of course, like neighing.

And he took a step forward which was a high kick. Immortelle noticed his disproportionately large red leather shoes.

They did not separate again.

With his light blue nylon cap, his gas mask and gloves – he manipulated blood, sweat and saliva, the three fluids of contamination as it was then believed – the colt would enter the "furnished apartment," as Immortelle's room was called, for whatever reason: to review the clinical sheet, to lower the mercury of the heavy thermometers, to retrieve a stethoscope he left behind, or to contemplate silently the yellow branches of the linden tree outlined against a uniformly gray sky.

Our breaths mingled, like two smelly animals; our bodies linked, locked together: a tangle of appendages and wrinkled clothes. Our skin was not the limit, nor our consciousness: everything became knotted as if scribbled incomprehensibly, furiously like an ideogram, without any wish but pleasure, without any goal but orgasm in its blurry immediacy.

We did not dare look at each other; we guessed each other's features, the shape of our lips. It all took place in the dusky and distressed shadows of the hospital.

First I felt him touch me as if absent-mindedly, then press my right ear, the earlobe between his thumb and forefinger, as if wanting to tear off a heavy earring or to know the real texture, the grain of my skin.

He anointed me with his saliva. I felt his disgust when he touched my wrinkles, the craggy dark stains that cover me, my veins visible and lazy, lacking the brutal force of the thick purple flow: swampy, dead streams.

"Desirous," I thought, "is he who flees his mother, as a way to return."

Besides, the bodies one loves are never real bodies, but rather others which the lover's imagination resurrects and projects.

Thus I saw myself naked, alighting from a very old train, a branch of purple flowers in my hand. What I now gave to the Horse was that imaginary body, weightless, almost astral, and not this flaccid bored mass of defeated tendons and uselessly alert nerves.

For a few seconds we occupied the totality of our bodies – no muscle forgotten, nor the slightest particle of skin outside of touch.

The Horse looked at me then, as if he recognized me.

We awoke from something. We returned to ominous wakefulness. We were the same as ever.

Everything about him was inept, misguided. Nevertheless, every gesture, no matter how awkward, radiated his precise strength, the reddish spark of energy that surrounded him like a halo in the fading light of the hospital.

My arms were two withered wings; he, a ridiculous centaur.

"Were you bored," was all I managed to say to him, "fucking an old lady?"

"No," he answered me curtly. "Now I'll be able to get a good night's sleep."

From that moment on, Immortelle had only one idea – fixed, by definition. Or rather obsession: she wanted to be rejuvenated. Go backwards in time, return to being who she had been, herself forty years ago, when she threw a blue and silver gala party to receive Bola de Nieve who had just returned from Paris.

She decided to resort, if it were necessary, to other medicines, to other sciences, to coincide once more with that image, though now past, of herself.

She spoke to no one of this project. Except, of course, the Horse.

Under the glass dome, flamingos or rainbows waiting in the rainy twilight, the discouraged inmates chatted about the loose *liaison* of Immortelle and the colt: the couple: a spirited sorrel – a wolf cub to some – and a demimonde mummified by the years and the potions, today inflamed – they believed – by injections of lamb placenta, or by concoctions of secret aphrodisiacs.

Some rumored that, among the offerings of an exiled monarch, the red-head had received a single-string pearl necklace: eighteen fatally grayish and brilliant baroque pearls fat as garbanzo beans.

In a photograph whose date and setting were uncertain, with a baffling seaside resort background, one could see her at the wheel of a Bugatti, under a broad-brimmed straw hat, pulling the soberly elegant necklace up and forward with her forefinger. Her dress: broken and concentric circles, in black and white cliché, or perhaps blue and silver. Her smile and eyes were unequivocal, the same as today.

Had the mischievous colt – some of them wondered – got wind of those pearls, like a drug addict who knows for certain where he will find his fix?

Others – in truth, very few – dismissed that interpretation of the facts as mean-spirited: it was simply love.

5

DOVES IN LIMBO

The meeting of the Horse and the saurian did not occur immediately, as the impatient reader, deformed by detected evidence undoubtedly expects. In stories, it's possible to withhold the worst, defer the unpleasant, and even cancel the ending, no matter how logical it seems. Mimicry intimidates more than one soul and turns his little tale into a hodgepodge of verifiable truths, although truths erased by the final period.

Speaking of mimicry: the saurian shaved off his beard in order to avoid Havanesque memories and left his hair very long. When he got dressed, he tied it at the back of his neck *à la catogan*. A solution of basil and purslane, which he put in his eyes with a dropper four times a day, dilated his pupils and sharpened his gaze so that he appeared to be contemplating things not on their flashy surface but in the indescribable center of their identity.

Dressed in silk, he left the red reefs. He strode over the burning sand and crossed the deserted highway – from far in the distance came the murmur of some trucks that he imagined polished like mirrors. He reached a town of zinc and wood whose houses were distributed around a gas station like tombs around a harbor church.

There were dovecotes everywhere: the stone gardens, the roofs of the few solid dwellings, even the wobbly tilted towers built of large boxes stacked on top of each other without being nailed or sanded. So great was the birds' cooing and amorous carrying on that the air seemed to be overflowing with wings, although it really was not: the fledglings made their first circular flight – reconnaissance missions – around the towers. The shanty town was empty: piled on the sidewalks of its only street were the rusted remains of automobiles and garbage cans in which no cats came to forage. There was a light breeze impregnated with the smell of garbage and other miasmas.

Someone.

At the end of the street, holding a toy hoop or perhaps a tire, was a child.

Two things astonished the approaching saurian. First, perched on the child's right shoulder was a small cockatoo with emerald wings and orange pupils. Second, the child looked Chinese, his head minuscule and round like a fossilized egg, or like a yellow balloon that swayed above his body, balanced on his atrophied vertebrae. Led by the hoop, he seemed to be floating far from such inhospitable surroundings. The saurian walked by him without so much as a nod.

There was an open door. He approached. The interior was almost dark, crammed with rickety furniture and plants that could only have been made of wax. An old woman sat dozing in a rocker beside a cradle that swayed to its own rhythm. On the clumsily hung wallpaper you could no more fit another empty space than you could set another picture frame on the lacy cloth covering the table in the middle of the room.

A young man in a doctor's coat leaned over the cradle. On the back wall thundered a massive clock stubbornly marking an ideal noon. Stuck in a sandbox, a dusty flag – the indecisive mascot of some ball club or the frayed emblem of a great nation.

"Good afternoon," he said, standing in the doorway.

The penumbra inside the room gradually dissipated: the old woman wore glasses and a gray coif; the picture frames were empty; beneath the cradle, suspended like a hammock on two iron hoops, was a dog; the plants were real. The loose threads of an embroidery fell from a lopsided loom. No one batted an eyelash. The rocker and the cradle continued to sway in unison, very slowly. The saurian waited a moment before suddenly crossing the doorstep and loudly proclaiming,

"I want water!"

They were still imprisoned in their awkward gestures: the old woman sat up straight in her rocker, adjusting the glasses with her tapered fingers so as to get a better look at the intruder; the man in the white coat turned toward the door.

He was the Horse.

"What gives you the right to enter a stranger's house?" the equine fired at him, slipping the stethoscope from his ears.

"I live on the reefs," he responded. "I know how to cure with herbs. And to rejuvenate. My name is Cayman."

"I was looking for you."

The Horse had come, summoned by the one hand-cranked telephone in the hamlet, to examine a stupefied infant, possibly the old woman's great-grandson and, like her, fond of young dove broth and snoozes.

Soon a huge gray carriage, reminiscent of the first class car on a train, with its flashy wheels and copper horn on the hood, came for the Horse; at the helm, the mansion's two impetuous official ambulance drivers: Socorro and Auxilio, AKA Help and Mercy.

Dressed in white, they were neat and starched, with a Prussian blue border on their square collars and the hems of their skirts.

The emblem of the Red Cross discreetly decorated their caps, which were held in place with enormous hairpins.

They covered their ears as if they were about to take a dive, and each one descended from her side of the car with a short leap from the driver's seat. There was a crow-like screech as they opened the back door and extracted a roll of canvas, which they immediately unfolded, between two wooden sticks.

"That won't be necessary," the Horse shouted to them from inside the hovel. "The cradle will serve as a stretcher."

And to Cayman,

"Come with me."

The great-grandmother watched them leave carrying the cradle, without turning her head, without the least expression. And she gave the rocker a good push with the tip of her toes.

As soon as they took off, the supposedly ataraxic baby took out an enormous rattle hidden in the cradle and began to wave it frenetically. It was a dried gourd, with little stones inside and black figures – salamanders and birds – drawn on the sphere. The noise was deafening. They had to close the cradle with a collapsible blue canvas hood. The angel with the rattle quieted down.

"We're from the south of Spain," said the ambulance driver who was at the wheel. "We're traveling across Cuba for processional reasons and now we're here, without knowing exactly why."

"In the interest of good," added the other. "In the interest of good."

The ambulance leapt and honked over the potholes in the road. Thus, they left behind the gas station, the tower and the naked blades of a windmill, a monastery in ruins, an old gypsy inn and a crossroads. A compass card, its names reversed like tongue twisters, the heirs of improbable Indians, pointed to the country house with the dovecotes and the coast on one side and, on the other, the large Moorish mansion of the morbid. The rest was uniform, veins of dry sand, porous bluish stones like lunar relics. The birds' passing was the sole incision in the silence.

From the front seat, Help and Mercy lavished gentle jokes and affectionate symmetrical attentions on the baby, who entered a state of flushed, furious euphoria, waving his blotchy red legs and arms and emitting a continuous high-pitched shriek in bebop rhythm.

The ambulance drivers took turns at the wheel, making frequent stops, on various pretexts, among them, to urinate. They squatted down, expelling a stream and an adage:

"Caring cures."

"Neither body nor soul exists."

No one spoke of anything but transcendent topics during the entire trip.

6

AND IF THIS WERE
A MERE SIMULATION?

With that case, the Horse had finished his round of patients.

In the vulgar mathematical accounting men make of time, only three days passed with their precise birds and the foreseeable decline of their sunsets; for Immortelle, for whom the Horse's absence was like a thirst, years had passed with their aging and fatigue, as they pass, recognizably, over the surface of men and things.

She devoted herself to waiting. But not to waiting while thinking about other things and sipping Anis del Mono, as one awaits a sailor who will return with his salty body. No: she waited in her armchair, sitting stock-still, intent on waiting as if concentrating on an intricate mental equation. She followed the colt's meanderings in the labyrinth of dry circumvolutions that was her imagination.

She visualized his tall figure, his enormous teeth, his metallic eyes. It occurred to her that the Horse might perceive reality as a sphere, enlarging the objects found on its edges – like all equine creatures, who see from the heights of their own size a skillfully sited ram and with this companion (an optical simulacrum) they traverse the solitary night, without the smell of fresh hay, enclosed among the four nailed boards of a box stall.

Immortelle sensed very close his centaur body in reverse, his torso of polished copper, the weight of his sex, his sinewy feet ready to arch so that he could thrust an impossible javelin.

Then she imagined him enveloped by a circle of animals devouring one another. A greenish and voracious Cayman was choking on a cobra that rippled in the hands of an Indian god as it swallowed a weightless hummingbird on a lump of sugar in the air; in turn, drawn by its phosphorescence, the bird gobbled up a firefly. The Horse centered this chain of swallowing animals-emblems: a circle of bulging eyes, claws, feathers and scales.

She saw him, finally, surrounded by geometric objects: luminous prisms and octahedrons endowed with thought.

"Enough dreaming, lady!" exclaimed a hurried nurse, tired of seeing her in such a cataleptic state that she couldn't get her to swallow her morning pill. "If you keep this up, in the clouds this way, you'll never get out of here! You gotta do your part!"

She awoke. She swallowed. She looked out the window at the sandy landscape, the old men in white pajamas marching, as if in a procession of Mercedarians, toward the glass dome, to sit on the benches, to attend the orange-colored migrations of the season.

Immortelle "floated" above it all, as the gypsies would say, without excessive suffering, and could absorb her medicines regularly without distorting the doses or breaking their bottles. The attendant – a great big gypsy who spoke Castilian Spanish, straightened his hair and always smelled of Camay – kept dodging her, leaving her for later, putting her offff for more urgent matters, until he forgot all about her.

Or almost did: he'd go by at seven in the morning, peer into her room, and when he saw that her hair had already been combed into a single braid which gave off reddish highlights, that she had blue mascara on her eyelids, wore fuchsia red lipstick, and was wrapped in a undoubtedly Chinese robe, he couldn't avoid the facile witticism and shouted out loud:

"Immortal!"

One night the dwarf cat returned – but completely changed. He entered by the window whipping his tail back and forth, furious because he wasn't allowed to sleep in the room, always hunting down the remains of corn flakes. For his name he soon deserved a Gallicism: Eternal Compagnon. So that he would not leave again. The little cat washed himself, taking no recess except for sleep, at which point he would snore: the sound was like that of very fine sand sifting from one end to the other in the emptied interior of a bamboo shoot. As soon as he heard the clatter of washbasins, or a clicking, or some deduction led him to realize that there was water, he would flee in terror.

And so it was that on the third day of the Horse's absence, the fragrant gypsy and his acolyte who obviously imitated his ovaloid gestures and tidy hair, appeared in the *suite impériale* – Immortelle's crowded dive. Amid much laughter, they were pushing at full speed a shiny disinfected bathtub, its prow in the form of a conch shell, pink and mother-of-pearl, like the iridescent throne of a Triton. A wooden platform, with four little oiled wheels, made possible that festive displacement normally reserved for the stretchers of the dying, with their attached transfusion apparatus.

"We're coming for your monthly bath," announced the attendant. "Do you prefer a brush or a sponge?"

"What does it matter?" replied Immortelle, who attested to the stigmas of time in her Japanese mirror. "I bathe myself every day without anyone's help. One thing's for certain: you will have to put me into that tomb of warm water. If I do it, and slip, I'll break everything. I prefer a sponge."

Thus, wrapped in an invisible shroud around the arms and feet, the bony bowed body was lifted by the smiling duo, a lock of red hair hanging from her occiput like a fiery mane, into the disinfected and shiny water.

"You'll forgive me," declared Immortelle, "if I don't soap myself. There are movements I find impossible, almost all of them. It's the fatigue."

"We're all tired, madame. Even the birds. Don't you see how they fall exhausted upon the dome and no longer travel in a straight line, in a single flight to the coast?"

"It's not the same fatigue," Immortelle protested. "Mine is otherwordly. As if it had no limits. Something that turns into the body itself, into the air I breathe."

"Like when you drink rum in the summer and then walk out into the sun..."

"And what's more," added Immortelle. "There comes a moment in which there is no difference between oneself and the fatigue. They are, or we are, one and the same thing. Then we console ourselves with images of past euphoria, of the body's remote joy...."

"What's most stimulating is to have the sea nearby," the big gypsy concluded, constantly lavishing his Castilian lisp.

"Or to be near someone with that energy."

The jokers continued to rub her with gusto, as if they were polishing a bronze skeleton – the sinister ornament of an ossuary – in the insular rococo style.

Distracted by the pleasant conversation, the rubbing duo splashed disgusting soapy water on the armchair that until then had been spotless, flooding, in passing, the mirror on the vanity and the jars of make-up, when they weren't inundating the rug upon which Immortelle would lie down to do her breathing exercises.

"The smell is the telltale sign," she observed, sinking into the lukewarm water, "that familiar stink of hospitals and operating rooms: they've put a little disinfectant in the bath water...."

"You're right," the acolyte admitted, "but very little and covered up by shampoo."

"This will not prevent," Immortelle continued ironically, "the body from continuing its process, which even in life progresses toward putrefaction."

Relaxation, a sense of well-being gradually came over her; in the few muscles she had left there was not the slightest tension... She saw the Horse leaping, heard his laughter, touched his mane...."

"Madame," the soapers shouted, "don't you go fainting on us!"

"You finally returned," was all Immortelle said when the Horse appeared at the door with a toothy and jovial horselaugh. "Alone I'm face-to-face with old age. I comforted myself thinking about a Poiret dress."

"I'm back, and in three days, as I promised you," the colt replied, and he gave her a kiss on the forehead. "And not alone. I bring you a man who cures everything with leaves and roots, and returns your wasted youth to you forever."

Surrounded by a whitish halo, saurian and proud, Cayman appeared at the door. His dilated, transparent pupils fixed on those of Immortelle, as if he were about to hypnotize her.

There was no time for more introductions. The diligent ambulance drivers arrived at the suite.

"Here he is," it was Help, raising up the baby and showing him to Immortelle: "we bought him especially for you."

"Good God!" Immortelle cried out, "he's real!"

"You've got to fatten him up," Mercy speaking. "He looks a bit sad."

"Let me give him a kiss and prepare him a bottle. Let's call the kitty over to entertain him. The two of them will be fine in the armchair. I'll sing him a cradle song a Cuban taught me in my youth: "*Duerme negrito*....""

"And we're off running," concluded the exacting ambulance drivers with identical gestures, as if one were no more than the reflection of the other. "There's a dying man whom we must return to joyous life."

"Or accompany," finished the Other, "without delay to the threshold of the Beyond...."

"Because there is a Beyond," argued the One.

"At least" the Other commented in greater depth, with a sigh, "the beyond of this side of the beyond."

They let loose a Draculesque horselaugh, which they had tried in vain to suppress.

Immortelle, the Horse, Cayman and one of the gypsies – the other was soaping in the next room – remained in the cubicle, contemplating the baby – now stiff and colorless – in the armchair, between two arabesque red and golden cushions, and the cat, who kept opening his mouth and puffing like a dragon spitting fire.

"We should go get some gifts," the Horse suggested.

"Useful gifts," Cayman added.

The baby remained motionless.

Suddenly, the same anxiety seized all four of them:

"My God...what if this were only a meticulously crafted puppet on a string, a mere simulation?"

7

THAT'S HOW IT ALWAYS IS...

They could not pursue such a crude inquiry. They were perturbed by the accusations, insults and offensive cries which those affected by the weakness fired at the nonetheless attentive therapy personnel not only prudent to the point of excess, but even affectionate.

Under the transparent dome, where the sounds from the five corridors wound up, the undertow from the commotion was unbearable.

"Leaving the hospitals of the Continent, where perhaps they'll one day find a cure, and burying oneself here seeking silence, to suffer this racket...," one of the old men bitterly complained.

The one next to him countered with resignation:

"That's how it always is...."

When someone, especially someone young, learns the nature of the malady from which he suffers, the texture of the poison that has invaded his flesh, he can react in one of two ways: from the repertoire of the stubborn murmur that stirs up and purges anything morbid come images of blood and semen: the clotted red of anger, or the soothing white of sperm.

Some of them rebel against everything, even against themselves, disregarding the prescribed dosages and divine will. They destroy, blaspheme, insult, abjure. There are those whose anxiety leads them to try to inoculate the healthy with pernicious leprosy: "I don't want to go alone," is their motto.

Others become withdrawn in thought, wall themselves up in an inaccessible muteness, inane aphasics mired in stupid somnolence as if they were mystics.

Something, however, joins those lost in thought and those who howl: the preoccupation with weight, the panic of becoming disembodied in life, victims of that irreversible muscular fusion whose etiology is an enigma: the malady itself, or the palliatives and placebos with which they try to delay its progression.

They hate – those who know them – Giacometti's rickety thread-thin figures heralding, unbeknownst to the maestro, the man of their tomorrow who is the man of our today: they move forward, skin and bones, fleeing the void. Or going toward it.

There were constant migrations along the corridors to confront the only functioning scale in the hospital and scrutinize it ounce by ounce, assigning it the objectivity of an artifact to evaluate the progress or recess – there was never any regression – of its lethal course.

There were some who, in order to give themselves courage or to put on healthy airs, plotted pitiful deceptions: weighing themselves early in the morning, before defecating, to add that laughable and fetid dead weight – or their underpants and socks – to today's calculation.

Others, with ostensible naivete, moved the indicating needle above zero, or stood on the scale leaning on their right leg, to unbalance discreetly the verdict of the numbers.

Fewer of them – it's true – after verifying the daily losses, abandoned that protocol, indifferent to the oscillations of the faithful: "In *la ronde* of the living and the dead one always get to dance with the ugliest girl...."

They all tried to attenuate loss with providential products to which they attributed the highest virtue: augmenting muscular volume.

They resorted to a viscous and sweet milky cream, rich in proteins, that tasted like malt or mother's milk.

One could also resort to a notorious lime and highly volatile powder, which needed to be dissolved in sugar water, used to restore athletes suffering from deficiencies and anorexics of all kinds.

Both products, in any case, gave the insatiable consumers the identical results: the runs.

Under the dome, as the sun set toward the beach, tinting the transparent windows as if they were stained glass, there appeared a short-haired, cautious, slow mannered old soul who seemed to study each gesture before executing it. His thin hands, nails cut short, were filled with newspaper clippings, a yellow notebook with graph-paper sheets, color pencils and a ruler.

"Are you noting down the frequency of bird flights, according to each species," the blonde asked him.

"No, I'm not only its victim, but the historian of the disease. I note down everything. One goes along learning little things. Ten years ago we knew nothing."

"And today?"

"At least the first symptoms, the rhythm with which it appears in a particular place, the distinct brevity of life."

"How butterflies appear and die instantly in the heat of twilight."

"Exactly..."

Like all closed minority societies, those weakened by the malady suffered from intransigent medical fashions.

The first of which there was any memory, according to the historian's data, was the cucumber method from China, a daily extract of that cucurbitaceous vegetable used by the wise men of the Empire to heal boils, which, in their herbal ideograms, were cinnabar erasures. Remissions were spectacular and ephemeral.

Herbal homeopathy followed next. The infected were inseparable from their notebooks with numbered Latin phrases, faded and moth-eaten like sorcerers' *grimoires*, and from their drastic little pills.

Vitamin C, it was upheld, in massive doses even healed tumors. The converts consumed it in raw form – before any pharmaceutical perversion – in great spoonfuls and at all hours. They prevented cramps with green clay in large shovelfuls. And watched movie comedies.

They wound up raucous and sleepless.

Then transfusions of contaminated blood became more widespread, supplying their bodies' failing defenses with others generated by a new though related immunity. The green medicine brought by Cayman was not far from being a new utopia. Perhaps that's why it was easily enforced, at least in the *suite*.

"And are you studying us," continued the blonde, "the way others do with lizards?"

"Yes, but with a difference. In what I study, in its clawing and turning, its cruel rage, its course toward nothingness, my own body is implicated...."

He organized the newspaper clippings, classified them in the yellow notebook, waved, and left.

∞ 8

**BLUE AND SILVERY
(FORTY YEARS EARLIER)**

Everything was silver, shiny, duplicated in a mirror three meters long with a chiseled frame: candelabra, lockets that were figures twisted like flames, sheltering a small bone in their breasts, vertical wall clocks, brocades, and even two roosters – *entre nous*, in poor taste – wrought in silver, which seemed to be dueling with their beaks, flying over the oval rosewood and glass table.

"It's just that I have," explained Sonia caressing her hair, "the Mexican malady," something that comes from the depths of time, from before time, and which cannot be avoided: the passion for silver that shines without dazzling, like a more dense, decanted mercury.

And glittering in the candlelight, her rings, her heavy bracelets, her necklaces of masks and hoops lavished, whenever she abruptly shook her head, an enervating tinkling – the sound of small coins thrown with fury against a gong.

She had been fascinated by his hands, the confidence of his gestures, the length and shape of his fingers, his ring finger and his middle finger wide apart, his skillful way of touching.

To receive that young architect, whom she barely knew, she had organized a party in which everything was silvery and blue, with the definitive exclusion of gold and its yellowish alloys, and tolerance of wrinkled purple, which fits so well with the insular night.

She lacquered walls, doors and piano with Prussian blue. Navy blue and cerulean for the orthogonal wood furniture. She dyed the curtains with a hue recalling the tribal tattoos of that desert and which she baptized Hoome. Her dress was indigo, her turban silver and Prussian blue.

The patio of the mansion – previously a town hall, and even before that, citadel of Mence's reign – was filled with giant ferns, malangas, tall sugarcane and bamboo, and even a bonsai plant, all of them so realistic that they displayed falling or withering leaves, or leaves stained gray by bird excrement. There were fresh buds blossoming and sickly tree barks, as if to denounce the vegetal passage of time, more abrasive in those latitudes in which everything is planted, blooms and rots in the wink of an eye. Or perhaps it was merely the mocking negligence of a part-time gardener.

Tall kerosene lamps illuminated the wise architecture of the garden – the excessive heat or the danger of burning mattered little – with their erect wicks and their stable blue haloed flames: the mist did not blow in.

The pianist, needless to say, wore a pastel blue tuxedo. He was a big fat bald dark black man, with a smile of flashing white teeth, a chubby-cheeked angel or baby. After a Versaillesque bow and a few virtuoso arpeggios for such short thick hands, he intoned: "Monasterio Santa Chiara..."

His voice broke as if he were crying or had just been crying. His eyes were two big round ivories – he was so ebony! – where the pupils ran from one side to the other, flustered billiard balls.

A woman plastered with powdered eggshell, or very pale, her long legs revealed by her open dress of tuareg silk-lamé and pheasant plumes in her turban, fan and shoes – sighed deeply and dropped onto a wicker armchair with its back in ellipse, like a Moroccan throne. She pretended to faint, so great was her emotion! She held stable, nonetheless, a glass of champagne, which she immediately drank.

The albino twins also dressed in blue. Grated blue. Yes: with a grater they had sprinkled indigo over white cotton material. How they danced for their age! Looking into each others' eyes and swinging their hips all over the salon. They opened their arms and their long skinny little fingers, which looked like porcelain asparagus about to break. Their tiny lacquered shoes with metal toes resounded like tambourines beaten by tiny soldiers with the string tensed to breaking point.

Besides that foreseeable and facile spectacle of the mirror reflection, they had filmed another, doubtlessly inspired in some mime: they tried to touch each other, but between the two rose a thick imaginary glass wall which they materialized with open hands and anguished expressions, delivering mute blows and trying to climb over.

"How identical they are!" observed a little woman with long hands and bulging eyes. "Especially this one!" And she began to applaud frenetically, overcome by an irrepressible nervousness.

"And what are you going to do when you grow up?"

"First of all," they replied in unison, "distinguish one from the other, not look at all alike. Be other...and after: good, just do good."

The woman with the bulging eyes applauded once more.

They all turned around to look at her, with a mocking little smile, or compassion.

A silence.

The musical eccentric undertook *J'ai deux amours*.

Sonia – to the architect –:

"He's Monsieur Julien, what do you think?"

"Of Monsieur Julien?"

"Yes, Julien Martinez Pidal y Ruiz."

"Unforgettable. But to tell you the truth, I'd rather be underground already."

"Suicide is a fashion, like any other. It will pass. Everything is ephemeral, even the desire to die."

"It's not that. I want to live underground. In a cool and quiet house, where you can hear the wind blow like sand and hail falling inside. Where lizards and birds enter and exit."

"Alone?"

"Yes."

The obese black man had created that devout silence, that incredulous withdrawal, somewhere between amazed and mournful – the stamp of any true revelation, as immediate as it may be, of the work of art, leaving the one who contemplates it submerged in an inexplicable absence, in a non-being similar to imbecility, aphasia or beatitude.

He had bluntly cut off the chitchat of the champagne guzzlers and the ferocious feathery fussing of the frivolous. Now, having torn from the petulant partygoers the respect that his lucid performance and the singularity of his voice required, forgotten by all the initial discomfort of his strange or grotesque presence, he could attack, without theatrical or vocal effects, in secret, almost in silence, as if sung softly to an overfed baby filled with mother's milk at island siesta time, his favorite lullaby:

Duerme negrito
Que yo va compra nueva cunita
Que va tene cascabel...*

From an emaciated waxen hand a champagne glass fell crashing to the floor in pieces.

But nobody paid any attention.

Sonia – after the applause, which followed the compactness of a silence –:

"Now I understand what my mother said: she had thanked God for having been born at a moment when she could still see Nijinsky dance. She had seen him at the end, before his madness, in a very short ballet that did not involve technical prodigies, neither caprioles nor rapid entrechats. Only the

---

* Sleep li'l black boy, I'll buy yo' new little crib, and yo'll have your rattle... (Translators' Note)

presence and the Hellenizing gestures of God's clown surrounded by some ecstatic nymphs. She was an expert at theosophy and had seen in that jittery angel a final avatar of Shiva, the dancing god. I am sure that I will never forget that lullaby, though much time may pass, though I'll never have anyone to sing it to.... And in that hole, what are you going to live on?"

"Fishing. It will have to be by the sea."

"And what are you going to do all day long, in a house without doors, where at any moment a scorpion can enter?"

"Paint. Paint animals on the stones according to their reliefs. In order to return to the origin of everything. Like those engineers who have listened underground to the vibration of the initial explosion, the birth of the universe."

"Will it be like the *so*(lar) key, when G remains in the air?"

"More like an echo," said the architect, "the echo of the Big Bang."

Sonia: "Are you going to dedicate your life to listening to a sound?"

The architect: "Any era houses many minor events, which occur on the edge of time and are invisible, or rather pass by their contemporaries like forgettable eccentricities or anecdotes. And, nevertheless, beyond major dates, invasions, massacres and wars, these other events are the ones that will change everything, that is, the future. The sound of the Earth is one of them."

Sonia: "That simple noise in certain antennae?"

The architect: "It can tell us where we live and when. Though, of course, not why."

The sweaty singer greeted them. With his little hands, chubby and awkward off the piano keys, he snatched a caviar and cheese hors d'oeuvres whose several layers alternated between Iranian gray and ivory white, from the tray which a servant – hair combed with brilliantine, obsequious and mannered like a musical hall chorus boy – passed around. Between flowers and felicitations, offers and fleeting kisses, he retired to a boudoir of deep Turkish cushions highlighted by silver filigrees and straight backed nickel-coated furniture whose legs shone in the dusky twilight that slowly took over the closed space of the fiesta, the successive salons and the garden, while the guests put down their glasses, picked up their hats and departed amid laughter, waving their hands to exaggerate how hilarious a discreet farewell gesture should be.

☙ 9
THE SOUND OF THE EARTH

They were not caves formerly inhabited and marked by the Indians; they were not industrial excavations that obeyed previous designs and the unlimited efficiency of machines; it was not the residue of the laborious leisure activity of unemployed and assiduous summer vacationers: it was a house, the brief utopia of an architect who considered all of nature a single living being, who spoke to the trees and knew their names, and maintained that there were stones with perfect triangles which no one had traced, others which could grow and, if the night was moonlit and calm, even dream.

He decided to live under the reefs, listening during the day to the sound of the tide and, at night, submerged in those strata, the almost imperceptible sound of the Earth turning, or the hum of the origin, the echo of the initial explosion.

Around then another architect had conceived a vast and transparent house, which unfolded over a waterfall, without destroying the stones or the trees, and in which one always heard the murmur of the falling water. Taking advantage of a chasm, as those in the region called the crater of a dead volcano, he built, excavated in the mineral itself, three superimposed circular rooms, which expanded their radiuses upward, like an emptied tower in granite; also, with identical proportions, a spiral staircase.

He accessed drinking water by boiling seawater and harvesting the steam in a still of his invention; his diet consisted of fish and algae.

The few pieces of furniture were amorphous and white; sand wrapped in sacks of a new material: plastic.

From the entry hole – both door and skylight – cascaded a plant of long purplish roots, the only one that had agreed to grow in this place. Those perfect vertical lead-like threads were interrupted at intervals by white star-shaped flowers, and a few lanceolated leaves which curved upwards in search of light.

The wind whirled around the three stories like a tornado. Up the craggy walls ran lizards, opening their gullets to distract a possible prey or to intimidate an imprudent enemy with the paralyzing dart of their tongues.

A coarse bird, who saw in the crater the possible concavity of a nest, ventured inside and there lost his way, crashed against a wall and fell, his neck broken, on the ground.

There the architect lived, apparently alone, projecting cities.

Until the hurricane.

The crest of the waves raised a white wall on the edge of the earth. The fish leaped somersaults in the air and fell among the reefs, asphyxiated. Birds never seen before were glimpsed fleeing toward the continent. A constant squeak, which seemed to follow the winding frame of the staircase, filtered into the ears of the beguiled builder. He took refuge under sand furniture, in the narrow upper circle. The house turned into a well of salt.

Exactly two days later, calm returned.

A woman in a car, turbaned and haughty, came looking for him, as if she had divined the worst. She was Sonia...

Strong sun, again.

Steady sea.

Perhaps resigned, without energies for a new undertaking, the architect abandoned everything. He contemplated for the last time the flooded crater and walked toward the car, without looking back.

But before, in a moment overtaken by anger, as if he wanted to destroy his patient work and leave evidence of his fury with the elements, he scrawled graffiti on the entrance to the crater: big ugly birds, an infernal lizard.

Then he yielded it all to the meticulous erosion of time.

10

BOTANICAL TERRORISM

We'll scrimp on details, which only serve to slow down the narrative, deflecting the reader's already flighty attention toward anecdotes and trivia.

In full possession of his pharmacopoeia – or his pontifications –, within a few days the Cuban herbalist converted therapists and male nurses, seduced attendants of all sexes, lavished advice and recipes, and multiplied irrefutable proofs of his science to such an extent that the formerly routine hospital had become a lush, brazen factory.

Soon they ran out of the dried herbs gathered in the stony landscape surrounding the small palace, promoted to cutting edge sanatorium. In the name of green science, they destroyed what little there was growing in the sand and, more than pharmaceutical missions, their expeditions were pure vandalism, assaults, roundups whose sole profit was knowledge and whose result was radical desertification.

Heartened by that hygienic utopia – and not, as some said, by the avid pupils of Cayman's eyes –, Immortelle renounced her cosmetics, which she declared "ruinous, tainted, and toxic," fed up as she was with bright colors and sticky gels, ready to return to a clear life, to harmony with air and light.

Infusions were the only formula that she found effective, whether one was sick or not. She consumed them excessively, submerged in boiling water with little impermeable bags, which afterwards she left on her dresser, along with the dried-out creams and the perfumes now devoid of fragrance.

"The nerves of leaves," one of the gypsies recited, "cure those of man; roots, having sensed the sound of the earth, reconstitute his vital energy."

And so, endowed with the noblest ideals, in the name of Health, but running out of green matter, Cayman and the Horse wound up involved in *botanical terrorism*, in total phytotechnical quackery.

Skeptics were excluded – those relegated to the ranks of regressive, or hooked on chemicals, or simply feeble old geezers – and they were deprived of all treatment, whether old-fashioned – classical medicine, with its tortures and failures – or current. Vitality was bestowed only on the adepts of beneficent Cayman and his equine accomplice.

They cleaned, disinfected and closed dermic stigmas – eruptions, pimples, boils, sarcomas, and mange – with tepid camphor compresses carefully applied, and they purged all sorts of dense, bloody or yellow humors with a concoction of soy, which purifies liquids and makes them as translucent and light as their source.

The practitioners spent their time scrutinizing urine and excrement, sweat and saliva. A meticulous science of signs, which excluded the reading of blood and took into account only certain materials, color, fetidness and precipitation, allowed them to determine unhesitatingly what needed to be given to whom, but above all – this, they said, is the beginning of any cure – when and how.

One morning a strident voice, like that emitted by a circus loudspeaker, or like the croak of a frog, interrupted the semiology of sediments:

"I will not accept, and this is a man of science speaking, that this stringent sanatorium, until now organized, often efficiently, surrender to the delusion of an herbalist!"

It was the old man, choleric and vindictive in the presence of the therapists, who talked about the heavenly bodies, opening his owl-eyes very wide, as if to defy Cayman.

Behind, pushing the wheelchair as always, calmly, despite the fierce philippic, came the blonde girl, formerly the transporter of her transfusion apparatus and now transformed into an adolescent with a graceful red beret perched on one side of her head over carefully set corkscrew-like locks gelled to perfect verticals. The sailor shirt remained.

"Now you, you and your buddy," he continued, "have alienated that poor old woman with your chlorophyllous philosophizing. But not me. May I tell you something? I've seen the stars and what happens at their center; I've seen thousands of galaxies spinning; I know their shape and I know where the universe comes from. That's why I'm not overawed by such nonsense and why you're not going to poison me with your medieval curare."

Without losing his temper, the Horse responded:

"We just want to cure."

"That's ridiculous!" retorted the astronomer.

The wheel chair made an abrupt half-turn. Taking off at full speed, the Pre-Raphaelite and the cosmologist fled up the corridor.

Through the glass dome, despite the daylight, you could see a chalky moon.

They did not stop.

They continued up the opposite, deserted corridor. As far as the linden trees.

To calm down after such an upsetting experience.

11

THE COSMOLOGIST'S DIARY

They've wallpapered the rooms: now the interior is light blue, a bit greenish, with bouquets of delicate flowers and calm flying seagulls – v's with curved and open wings – against a background of distant mountains.

A nearly bald old woman wearing a red plush housecoat is curled up on her bed beside an identically red Bakelite table, on which there's a neat row of oranges and bottles of orange juice.

They've lacquered the doors in greenish gray; the new furniture is made of fake leather and stainless steel. No matter where you look, except for the cracking ceiling, the floral pattern on the wallpaper is repeated, eliciting the same obsessive question every sleepless night: how many are there, in all the rooms or in the whole hospital, how many seagulls, how many little flowers, how many background mountains? Ad nauseum.

On the speckled turquoise linoleum floor, one can imagine the furious ebb of waves, the figurative dexterity of a Japanese master, cumuli-nimbi seen from a plane, a turbulence of tungsten or helicoidal galaxies in formation.

The noise: neither that of transfusion carts nor of wash basins clattering, nor of demented or pained shouts but a unanimous harangue from the continental television system that someone had the bright idea to install, its channels blasting in every room day and night with different vociferations and ghetto songs howling and clashing constantly. No one watches it. In every room its images prompt blue reverberations that intensify during the night when the large lights in the corridor are turned off and the only one left on is the minuscule red bulb over the door of one of the rooms – the sign that the nurse is there.

Sometimes cathodic chance synchronizes the rowdy diversity of those images; then, in all the rooms at once, in living color on all the screens, the same Indonesian monkey grabs hold of lianas that are electric cords and little tubes for probes and transfusions, the same white masks, the leap to trap an escaping infant; an Indian ballerina smiles, pounding the floor with her feet, golden bracelets, her small delicate hands playing little cymbals, you can feel the warm air, southern air from beneath a spreading tree as opulent and tangled as a city.

A *cantaor*. Broken voice, Flamenco lament. Someone changes the channel. Image and sound pulverize once again.

*

Being sick means being connected to various machines, vials of white liquid thick like semen, measurements in mercury, fluorescent charts on a screen.

The cure is a breaking of connections, of nexus, the body is free and autonomous, the sheets thrown off.

The astronomers saw celestial bodies, incandescent or porous spheres traversed by cataclysms of carbonic clouds and surrounded by splendid or glassy rings; for the cosmologists it was the same as for the sick: they connected us with machines in which the stars are falling ciphers – invariable and meager news from the universe.

*

A healthy, apparently blonde woman who was admitted yesterday promised to take me out for walks. Soon I'll be able to express my thanks to a machine that synthesizes sounds and which I had to invent, since these scientists are such prudes. The blonde is almost a child; it would be wonderful to touch her, trace the outlines of her body very lightly with my fingers, breathe her, feel how her insides pulsate – through her nose, her mouth, her anus and her sex.

A nurse goes by to inspect the nasal probes – don't let them fall out! –, take blood pressures, pulses, and temperatures. Her voice is soothing, rather naive; her bobbed brown hair makes her look like a *garçon*.

The room, Immortelle's *suite*, is still packed, despite the rule of one visitor per patient, something that she really is not.

Now, when the television quiets down, you can hear a distant murmur, as if loud bells were competing with nearby ambulances, the traffic of an improbable city.

The visitor arrives, intimidated by the asepsis in the vestibule and the fumes of disinfectant in the corridors, or by the dizzying repetition of bouquets and ugly birds and, exhausted, he sits in front of a sick man stunned or still prey to a recurrent hangover from the anesthesia, or perhaps bewildered by nature. So the visitor remains silent, until an ill-humored attendant ousts him under the pretext of an intravenous.

When the sick man wakes up, or returns to consciousness between two cataleptic seizures, he has the immediate impression that he's been the object of a wake; still lingering in the air is the grieved emanation of a presence, something undeniable and vague, like the odor of chrysanthemums long since removed.

*

Here, cutting one's nails and, even more, shaving, turns into a real feat of precision, so much so that there's an enormous fear of cutting oneself, spilling the blood's poison on some object, on a cloth that might come in contact with another's skin.

The illness has reduced me to this wheelchair. I'm a hodgepodge of bones and jaw turned inside out, a living Cubism, but I've seen what's been seen by few men since the scrutinizing, distant and patient Chinese who'd already observed it with their astronomical "lens": the explosion of a supernova. They saw it through the ideogram *pi*; I, in the midst of an austral night. We were watching the fastidious observation program from The Chair, thinking about something else, sheltered by the concave and total silence. Suddenly one of the astronomers gave a shout: at the edge of the sky, in the interstellar gas, the diffuse plasma of the cosmos, something had exploded with an inaudible, immense, and distant orange and violet bang, something nonexistent for millennia and whose explosion was reaching us today. Chemical twilight, crab turning with open pincers, incandescent aurora borealis.

*

I think, undone.

*

Identify yourself completely with something: with fatigue. So that between us there are no edges. We absorb each other into a morbid unity, like two amoebas devouring one another, sick and insatiable.

Now there are no spectators. No one who watches or judges the other; nor is there a different state, object, or being to face. Everything fuses or fades in the same thirst for unity.

12

THE BATTLE BETWEEN
HORSE AND CAYMAN

One morning in mid-summer, Immortelle got up as wizened and wilted as ever; but there was a noticeable difference: she wanted to live.

She slid her waxy feet honed as the hands of the dead into some slovenly red silk slippers, hung up the everlasting housecoat...and ran to the mirror. When she looked at herself full face and twice in profile, it was impossible to refrain from grimacing in disgust: so many tasteless, toxic, urticant or vomitive potions, all for nothing.

She was about to go back to bed, where she drew out her days leafing over and over again through the same fashion magazines, so old that they were once more at the cutting edge of design, when she was arrested by a detail in her image: her lower eyelid, previously traversed by a network of minuscule wrinkles, was now smooth, as if an invisible hand had stretched it towards both sides of her face, top and bottom.

She smiled. She did not know what to think. And she took her first sip of breakfast: a juice of natural soy procured by Cayman – in exchange for God knows what defloration – from the turbaned Malaysian dealers swarming in the precarious island port.

The next day – now this was incontestable – it was her hands. First, the nails: the moons were growing; then the phalange of those fingers that were furious claws; the skin was smoother, its deathly tone was changing, the bone was becoming hidden.

Rejected as a weird object by the medical personnel at the hospice, "an inveterate utopian, or a delirious do-gooder like everyone else from his country," Cayman was nevertheless tolerated as a long-term visitor or temporary resident: Immortelle paid a hefty weekly fee.

The Cuban herbalist went out in the early morning to listen to the lunar silence, the island's volcanic vibration, and to gather those roots feeble as pistils that live in the interstices of the petrified lava penetrable by fire and dew, both of which can be found there. He returned to the colonial mansion with dilated eyes – crystalline circles of invisible stretch marks – and the penetrating gaze of one who has seen day being born.

Feet wet, head damp, he carried the roots carefully placed in a little transparent plastic bag, like the ones used to transport small red fish.

When he arrived, he immediately looked for the glassy blue Dutch mortar – trefoils and coats of arms – that he kept hidden in a cupboard, and he smashed the tender herbs with a pestle moistened with anis. Holding that cloudy, cloying juice that resembled horchata, he ran to the *suite impériale*, Immortelle's room.

She was waiting for him with a towel soaked in lavender water, which she held with arms opened. Since by that hour her vermilion hair fell to her waist, she looked like a pious, though stupid, virgin from an altarpiece in some mountain village.

This time, when he handed her the potion, Cayman was the one to be surprised. He could not believe what he saw, nor had he ever thought that, even with the best of luck, the green medicine would yield such stunning results.

He looked at her carefully, first out of the corner of his eye, and then very close up, so that he could study her in detail. The most impressive things were her lips, the wings of her nose, the now strong outline of her once scrawny chin.

Cayman could not contain his happiness:

"It works!" he shouted. "It works!" And he covered her with kisses.

"I had found that out as well," she added tearfully. "But I said nothing so that people wouldn't take me for a crazy old woman."

She pulled off her worn-out slippers and, like a child showing off his scars, she held out smooth feet once wrinkled and bent: even the soles had changed.

Now she was the one to kiss his hands. She was still too overcome for words.

They celebrated with swigs of parsley juice.

Excited by the miracle, with the strength of his arms made robust by the sea and the pestle – we Cubans forget certain manual hobbies –, Cayman set aside in a corner everything in the *suite impériale* that could serve to remind them of discredited traditional medicine that was toxic and gave rise to more ailments than it was supposed to heal. Then, with an arrogant gesture, as if he were throwing a cape of lights over a bull bleeding to death, he spread a Manila blanket over that outlandish therapeutic sculpture upon which one could make out (beneath the fringe and the large exquisitely subtle flowers) transfusion hooks, empty hemoglobin vials, stethoscopes, and syringes.

They increased the pace of the treatment.

Now there were two mugs of frosty broth that the fasting candidate threw back her head to swallow in one gulp; she completed that regimen with frequent flexions, deep breaths of early morning air and slow exhalations to expel the invisible dross that clouds one's being.

Amidst such ardor, splendid birds in heat flew through the window, circled the intricate Murano lamp – Immortelle's latest acquisition – and left again, perhaps proclaiming the news of a tinkling ornamentation.

So great was the euphoria over the stretching, the sudden enthusiasm over return to the always more clement days of yore, that Immortelle adorned herself with a wax gardenia and lifted her reddish locks, reproducing in detail the legendary capillary structure of the Lady from Shanghai.

Help and Mercy, the diligent ambulance drivers, spent the morning applying their makeup so as to carry out painful humanitarian missions of the afternoon; the Horse had retired to the peninsula for a few days for an intensive course on the enigmas of the blood; the Pre-Raphaelite blonde had been discharged and, struck with wanderlust, she appeared only now and again, while the astronomer had locked himself in his cell on bread and water in order to write a diary about the end of the cosmos and its metaphor: illness.

Fortunately, no one was in the colonial mansion except the routine therapists, always apathetic, or in any case indifferent to the squeezing and stretching of an eccentric old woman and the sermonizing of her personal herbalist.

"Doctor," she told him with emotion, "Words fail me, I don't know how to thank you for what you've done for me. I'm the woman I was before... Or almost..."

She was wearing, solely to please the phytopractitioner, a dress with golden rectangles, eyelets, bows, and hieroglyphics that she'd found at the bottom of the trunk. And, exposing the wax gardenia, she had coiffed her head tightly with a hat à la Velázquez. There was no make-up left for her cheeks: she gave herself a few slaps that brought back the blush of times past, that fresh pink with mother-of-pearl streaks which painters of municipal portraits achieve with the color tube opportunely labeled "flesh."

"Yes," she added, "even my voice is changing. Less nasal. Don't you think? The voice changes the most; the voice is what you forget the least. I still remember the voice of a Cuban who sang at my house."

"We're only beginning," Cayman explained. "We have to follow through with the infusions to empty the body."

"Empty the body?" Immortelle was surprised.

"Yes. Plants, whose growth follows the seasons and the natural equilibrium, utilize, above all, the void they allow to remain between the leaves and which they only border or festoon. Man, however, from birth to death, does nothing but fill himself with impure foods, poisoned air, and things that accumulate, thus distancing himself from the void, which fills him with terror."

Immortelle adjusted her cap and looked at Cayman, but out of the corner of her eye and in the mirror, suggesting that in the baroque attire with which she had decked herself – all those scallops, spirals, and gildings, all those bugle beads with their funereal black brilliance – you could glimpse the reverberation of a different vacuity.

"'Every void,'" Cayman asserted, "'every absence, is a beginning and a path of abstraction and of movement, since it proposes a container, a form to the possibility of a content. Everything that is full is inert.* The void is an essential condition of movement and life.'" "But we have to be realistic, Madame," Cayman continued, suddenly changing his tone. "We still have to shape the breasts and recover the essential: the breasts. To strengthen them, they'll need to be massaged with acacia petals. Some watercress and blackberry brandy wouldn't be a bad idea from time to time...

The breasts? What can I tell you? Flabby. They fell like two maracas on the spines of corseted metal as soon as that poor woman unhooked the suffocating scaffolds of her dress. She picked them up with cupped hands to show them to Cayman, who unhesitatingly began to touch and weigh them, even pinching their sad nipples to see if he could make them a bit erect.

She felt pain when he squeezed her, but there was barely a flicker on her face, as, in order to hide the joyful reverse of such

---

* Claudel, sent by Héctor Bianciotti. (Author's note.)

ardor, she submitted docilely to the herbalist's large mitts, and sank into the voluptuous sensuality of obedience.

Without meaning to, guided by touch, Cayman moved to her stomach, her hips. Despite the absence of the firm mold of her mythic – since distant – youth, something – but what? – remained of the marmoreal volume of yore.

Cayman began to massage them, sculpt them as if they were clay. Immortelle allowed herself to be manipulated: she was a damp mud doll conquered by the skill of the potter. She scrutinized him from head to toe in the mirror. In silence. Hiding her pleasure. Almost with fear.

They looked at each other face to face for the first time, as if to become conscious of what they were doing.

"Did we say something?" Cayman asked, intimidated by his own daring, or pretending to be. "Or did we say nothing?"

Immortelle hesitated an instant, before responding:

"Nothing."

The potter continued shaping, lower and more earnestly. Now it seemed that he was trying to resuscitate the animate flesh with the digital pressure he applied in circles and with occasional slaps that occurred accidentally despite such great and such gentle precautions.

Immortelle softened totally, surrendering wholly to her sculptor.

She sighed. She moaned. A strange relief traversed her from head to toe.

"Enough," she pleaded. "Enough."

But Cayman didn't stop. On the contrary, he accelerated his manipulations.

At that point the Horse arrived.

He attacked kicking, and so furiously against the quasi-fornicators that they ended up: Immortelle with an opera finale shriek, against the three-paneled mirror, which she hurled to the floor, along with her combs, dryers, perfume sprays, and herb jars; Cayman, face down against the pile of medical junk that he'd just finished hiding.

Let's weigh the abilities of the two opponents on the scale of zoological rage:

— a horse can kick a Cayman to pieces, or better yet, rear up on him, asphyxiating and compressing him until he vomits his own green saliva;

— a Cayman can, with one somersault, trap a horse's hoof, clamping it in his snare-like jaws, thus immobilizing the horse until it dies.

As always happens with predictions, literary or not, the action unfolded in an entirely different manner.

"Before I die," the Horse managed to say, "I'll see your blood spill on soil."

"And I'll see," answered Cayman with a residue of assurance, "not only your blood but also your brains."

Help and Mercy, back from a charitable expedition, found them. They were emblems of constellations, twisted and blurred, drowned in the starry dust of their commingled bloods.

"My God!" Help exclaimed. "And with the linoleum so hard to clean!"

Immortelle, as was her duty, had fainted.

13

THE COSMOLOGIST'S DIARY

Two black male nurses pass, pushing an empty gurney. No: they're conveying a starving baby doubled up and unconscious beneath his sheets and blankets, his right eye covered by an enormous tuft of cotton; it's held in place by a cross of adhesive tape.

*

Assume fatigue to the maximum: even ceasing to write, ceasing to breathe.

Abandon self. Allow cessation of being.

*

Two old men are curled up one against the other, whispering to each other, seated in the long corridor. Thinning hair, gray loose fitting coats seemingly too large for them. In this heat. They look toward the white light, toward the linden trees. What more can I say about this instant of absence, in which nothing is truly present? A moment that barely is one and that exists only along its edges, detainment in which duration has been arrested, like an animal caught in ice.

A distant noise and one thinks of a barking, of a duck piercing the total silence as it takes flight; but the sounds form part of the silence, merge with it, mark it without annihilating it. Nothing is actualized.

There is no live place, only a figure outlined, fixed, like a drawing, the representation of an absent presentation. The bend of the park is there, like an object that cannot be modified, the opposite of those drawings in which movement has been captured in a way that makes the entire outline seem about to shift.

Here, I write, in this absence of time and place, in order for that negation to be stated and for everyone to feel within himself that same motionless deprivation of being.

*

A herpes on the eyelid, hidden when my eye is open, an incurable crack in the corner of my mouth, harmless stigmas, insignificant heralds of the irreversible that nature conceals in her extreme perversion: it is from nature, and not his precarious knowledge, that man derives his malignancies. A scratch a day, something that can be concealed by the lightness of the quotidian, a trivial morning alert in the mirror: never a blow, a frontal attack that could induce the body's self-defense. The naive fool rots unawares.

*

Sick is the man who examines his past. He knows – suspects darkly – that no future awaits him, not even that wretched one of attending events, of being present, though mutely, at his unavoidable succession. He surrenders then, meticulously, to arranging the preterit: with great ingenuity he shuffles causes and consequences, with obstinate recurrence he expands or evokes certain events, reducing others to trivialities, asks himself why some of the most memorable are obviously insignificant and even rather common.

One who is hopelessly ill laments his inability to forget the way he should; he would like to pass his time in total clarity, reduce his days to two or three essential syllables, which would be meager ciphers engraved on the inside of a ring, the invisible mark of his passage on Earth, the guarantee of his singularity.

For him, the present is a body in pain, is the impossibility of pushing that pain aside, of forgetting it in some dark corner like a rickety piece of furniture, like an old instrument whose enjoyment we've worn out and whose harmony marks only a childhood of imposed rules, efforts and repression. The future, by definition, does not exist. He moors the past, then, to things that he cannot recover, gradually immobilizing it like a tightening net; his memories make him believe that those things are purely objects to be played with, arranged, repaired, regretted, like the indecisive lines of a sketch; in reality, they're the recent ruins of a failed representation and gradually they devour the one who recalls them, a slow leprosy that annihilates and corrupts him from head to toe until he's converted into the organic ruin of a pious, putrid designation.

*

God is prodigious with atonement, to the ridiculous extremes of mockery when it comes to so-called old men, those who forever have lost their energy and their will. The funniest thing about this blunder, or rather design, is that the victim is perfectly ignorant of God's error, and of the code of prizes and punishments, reprimands and recompenses that governs his damnation.

These excesses of the sinister – also, it must be acknowledged, of the marvelous – are God's alone. One might even presume that they're His true signature.

*

Amid mounds of stone, large gray or yellow layers of sand. Strange, twisted trees, stripped of their leaves by the wind. The islands are rafts floating defenselessly, a colossal gust unties them and carries them to the other shore of the ocean, and there it scatters them, hurling them like Yaquis on the streaked blue of a floor tile, or into the carbonized, empty shell of a volcano. The melted stone, hardened and melted again as the millennia pass, sparkles on the macadam's morbid black reflection.

*

Slogan for the days to come, for the time I have left: PRACTICE NOT BEING.

*

The mass of mountains rising above the sea in the background – the islands are peaks filtered by the foam – is pierced everywhere: a network of underground rivers, a terraced perspective of corridors that simulate the interruption of a mirror, a double image whose silence makes it impossible to attribute an origin.

The cavities of old craters open without contour or relief in the middle of the flat rocky ground; stones fall from those enlarging orifices with a diminishing dull sound like a giant funnel in an abyss.

*

When the lack of energy assails, rather, when it gradually and slyly takes possession of the body, each day one loses the ability to do something, a gift expires or deteriorates, a memory is corrupted, a proper name is distorted. Our handwriting, for instance, once stable and uniform, in which our thoughts linked effortlessly and which was as legible as the score in the phrasing of a great pianist, today wanders from the line, trembles, exaggerates periods, accents, pennants, tildes. It's all a blot, a huge, incongruent crossing out, a vicious crossbow.

The amoeboid letters arise on their own, with no hand to curb their oily expansion. A bird of prey, greedy for our very waste, hides in each stroke.

I open the windows so I won't think about what will happen when the lack starts to increase: the air is motionless, does not enter, seems to be weighed down with a feeling of bitterness and desolation.

What's difficult is to think about something else, to move onto something different, without the threat, without the lurking image – Death – returning.

*

It seems that on other islands, on the rocky ground marked by some detufted palm trees – but evincing water and life – people have built cube-shaped, elongated or pyramidal whitewashed houses, the only forms that erosion will not reduce to the indescribable, the only colors that return light, breaking up the landscape with that figure of former fire, ruins of a ruin, residue of what had always been the result of a disaster.

I surprise myself evoking a body in the midst of all those erasures, those blottings and negations of life. A slender body swimming in a deep, transparent blue mozaic pool. The swimmer is black; he has firm buttocks. He dives: I'm splashed with cold water.

*

Pain deep in my eyes, as if it were about to snow, which is impossible here. Or worse: as if someone had a rag doll that was an effigy of me, and he were sticking pins in it to provoke my blindness and hasten my end.

*

It's a question of measuring the temperature of the ragged distant clouds of gas that are found in the dawn, at the edges of the cosmos. If by a millionth of a degree this temperature is higher than everywhere else, it will be proof of the Big Bang.

*

True hell will consist in there being *something*–whatever that might be–after death, in death not being a cessation, a total rest.

*

One collapses in fever: trembling, fainting and diarrhea...and continues to live. Each time the crises are deeper, they dilute the humour in one's veins, soften the marrow in one's bones. But the spells pass.

The body is emaciated, exhausted.

One should write a breviary: *On the difficulty of dying.*

14

LUNAR BEES
(FORTY YEARS EARLIER)

"Wait," Sonia shouted, "don't go! We have to end the night in a big way and way up high!"

The staggering drunks looked at one another in astonishment, wondering what was this new madness. Most of them rejected the proposal, claiming they were out of breath, had headaches and other alcoholic traumas that failed to hide their apprehension about ascending.

The architect remained, however, as did the albino girls, two night-owl musicians (who had already stayed up the night before), a few fervent servants, and those festive fanatics for whom daily amusement is an irrevocable duty. Excusing himself with countless cajoleries and hand wavings, the musical Cuban eccentric withdrew.

"I'm going to my room on an urgent mission," Sonia informed them. "I'll be right back."

When she returned, the troupe of awkward but elegant and fearless followers squeezed into three shiny polished cars, raised as if on stilts over tires inflated to the point of bursting.

The exhaust pipes, enormous and twisted trombones, trembled. Over tone-deaf songs and drunken laughter you could hear the hoarse horns, the engines coughing: the air filled with tiny finely outlined amoeboid black clouds that the albinos began to sniff with pleasure:

"There's no perfume," they exclaimed, "like modernity!" And they inhaled carbon dioxide until they filled their lungs.

Then Sonia drove out her blue Bugatti, steering with her gloved left hand, her right crammed with jewels, raised in a recruiting gesture to give the "Follow me" signal to her unconditional devotees.

In those days there were not many buildings on the islands, and the simple white houses clustered in the valleys, connected by a solar, indigo blue coat of arms with six petals, did not add up to a suburb. And so the bewildered caravan, lined up behind the Bugatti, soon found itself on the side of an arid hill whose slope, noted the architect, was outlined so perfectly that it seemed an engineering feat rather than a natural incline.

The lights in the hamlets were still lit, oil lamps whose wicks emitted blue sparks that, from a distance, looked like an intricate galaxy.

The abrupt slope that followed was covered with ordinary marble slabs like tombstones, but bursting through cracks left by the imperfect union of the stones were abundant brambles, reddish bushes, tall grass where a herd of sheep grazed during the day. Now they slept peacefully beside the road, submerged in their woolly night.

Curled up upon a hillock in their midst, all vigilance cast aside, the shepherd also slept, wrapped in rags, face up with his hands opened, his sandals ever bound to his feet.

The shouts and blasting of horns sent them all scattering. The goatherd leapt to his feet and stood making sleepy gestures that, though eloquent, were anything but auspicious for the confused retinue of joyful noisemakers.

The climb continued for a long stretch, but soon they had to halt everything. One of the sightseers – salmon tailored suit and turned-up nose – was seized with a vomiting spell: they worried she might stain the doors of the *cabriolet*. The twins immediately suggested they leave her on the side of the road.

"The ragamuffins will soon give her goat cheese!"

The architect had to intervene so they could continue their brazen enterprise.

When the retching subsided (the heavings were contagious) they proceeded to tackle the flanks of another hill, higher and steeper than the previous one: the route turned into a rocky zigzagging road. They had to stop from time to time and push aside the sharp rocks in front of Sonia's car that were blocking the way.

Nonetheless, they went at top speed. So fast that the women resorted to their thick goggles, held up by black elastic, and their sturdy aluminum helmets, now prisms where the beams from the steering wheel were reflected.

Nothing more opportune.

The convertible's hood squeaked, the tires skidded in the dust, the brakes gave way and they burst out shrieking: a colossal cloud of bees – incongruent in this place devoid of flowers or light – attacked the convoy so viciously that it seemed to be obeying an order, its robotic, blood-thirsty warriors defending a sacrosanct and secret territory.

On their black-striped golden bodies the eyes occupied the whole head; the wings vibrated endlessly with a buzz intolerable to man; they swarmed so thickly that they blocked out all possible vision.

The bees enveloped them completely as if wanting to asphyxiate them. They had to raise the windows and, suffocating, use their hats to kill the intruders, which had already infiltrated the car.

"They're poisonous!"– predicted the woman with bulging eyes.

And a musician:

"They're humming up a storm! They vibrate in three successive notes, as if they knew the musical scale...."

The drivers turned off lights and engines.

They remained in silence amid the myriad sharp wings, perverse polyhedral eyes, legs and antennae.

Some went to sleep. Others smoked – which poisoned the little air remaining –; the twins swallowed horse pills for sleeping that they always carried secretly, just in case, and fell into each others' arms, snoring in fetal position.

Thus they remained until Sonia, without knowing why, thought of turning on the headlights and shifting their position to make rapid signals to an oncoming truck that was rushing toward them.

Then the detestable hexapods hastened in unison to plant themselves in the road bathed in the intermittent light. The route was a honey-colored pool that animated almost imperceptible movements, yellow animal tremors.

It wasn't difficult to crush them and continue on.

"They're lunar bees," the architect explained. "They're conditioned to orient themselves according to the milky white light of the moon and not sunlight. They produce the double of the classical bees; their little cells are pentagons, an architecture of which man is still ignorant. They build their beehives up high, to be closer to astral tides. They are no friends of man...."

"And how do they live?" the musician asked.

"No one knows for sure. All we know is at a given moment there arrives an elderly queen who has reigned perhaps in another place and over other workers. The young drone feeds her an herbal extract (green honey that strengthens and transforms her). Then the queen leaves, we don't know if to die alone or to reign over another hive."

Night had fallen when they reached the top.

A rock garden erased the road, stones that rose over a still river of lava and which looked as if they had been carved by sculptors, so much so that their edges and textures were visible. Some, spherical and polished, depicted bushes of basalt, hedgehogs, giant ebony sponges; upon others the imagination could project titans, cripples begging, chessboard bishops and even nymphs escaping their rapists and whose fingers were turning into leafy laurel branches.

They projected uniform grayish shadows over the pebbles.

Everyone got out.

They scattered in boisterous bands, like birds liberated from captivity.

The architect remained alone, waiting for Sonia. The carousers moved away down the mountain, exploring stone labyrinths.

There was a great silence, faintly interrupted by a distant guitar. Finally there was the sound of the first car's door slamming.

Then Sonia appeared, wrapped in an indigenous rag: interlacing lizards now embroidered only by the old women in an abandoned village. The moonlight made her look very pale; her reddish hair formed a flaming crown around her face; those dark eyelids, the opal yellow eyes, her absent gaze as if true being were elsewhere.

She was walking barefoot. In her right hand she carried, like a martyr, the testimony of her torture, a vanity mirror that she held by its silver handle twisted in the form of a snake.

The architect: "What's this for?"

Sonia: "Mercury, also lunar, concentrates and reactivates white dust. Dust is the quintessence of leaves. And leaves are life."

The architect: "And this is why we came up here?"

Sonia: "Yes. Heat, the strong sun and excessive light are bad for this fragile snow. Here it's volatile and energetic, and it evaporates in the body. It proves..."

They inhaled calmly, one by one, the parallel lines of that light frost.

Birds passed, perhaps disoriented.

The somnambulistic repetition of a single guitar note sounded in the distance.

The mirror reflected their faces close together.

One more line. Until they perceived those stones like something factitious, without the slightest solidity or substance; a scenery with neither volume nor background, conceived by some madman who fancied himself an aesthete, and ready to collapse or vanish.

It was she who grabbed his hands – desiring them more than anything, more than the rest of his body – and placed them on her breasts. At first intimidated, he followed the magnetic lines of that firm body, perfect in its volumes, in its entrances and salient parts: an inhabitable and secret place he discovered gradually, groping his way, a refreshing refuge. He felt for the first time, in the fusion of their bodies, the nocturnal presence of the volcano, the murmur of the earth: the river of magma – the planet's blind incandescence – flowed deep.

It was already dawning when they descended. Sonia always in front, the others, rather than consciously following her, were a line of drowsy sleepwalkers, zombies.

It was at the curve of the bees where Sonia's Bugatti lost its brakes.

The car was reduced to a charred heap.

She emerged unscathed.

From that day on she was plagued by a nickname that little by little she accepted, until it became her real name: Immortelle.

15

THE COSMOLOGIST'S DIARY

There are days when we wake up and the energy is there. Not beside the bed, like an assiduous sentinel, nor facing us, like a persistent apparition, but within us: the lungs saturated with sea sediments, with the living air of the island night, while the arteries pulse with blood as alert, fresh, light and intoxicating as newly distilled alcohol.

Excessive colorful birds appear, turning linden trees into the miniatures in Persian tapestries. Debut of warblings, tiny sulfur whirlings – baby canaries – around the glass dome.

The first thing that emerges for one who knows that sooner or later he is condemned, is the inexplicable and urgent need to *do something*, to produce with his hands, or with his corroded intelligence. He eludes the pure air of the distant tide, ignores the circling of the birds; he wants only to mark, to put his stamp on the real.

Another desire surfaces – this one unrealizable – : to raise his arms very high, fill his lungs with air, hold it a moment... Then, lowering his arms, to expel the noxious, lethal germ.

I immediately conceive of an astronomical project: commerce with the universe saves one from pettiness, shields one from the unimaginable dimensions of the trivial.

They – who? – gave us life as a precious gift which we never requested and in the giving of which – birth – we did not participate.*

We've reached the point of forgetting life, or considering it something transparent, imperishable: our senses distract us from its calm flow beside us, this muddy current in which we are actually submerged.

Until suddenly, one day like any other, we realize that the gift, the free offering we were enjoying is going to be taken from us: that day is foretold by a lack of energy, an inevitable loss of weight, an uninhabited color the sun cannot eradicate.

If we look at ourselves in a mirror without thinking – for example, while walking toward the glass dome, in the mirror of that vivacious old woman whose door is always open – , what we see is chilling: a frightful scarecrow scurrying along, with sunken cheeks, bald head, sharp nose and blackish lips. The figure is surrounded by a large paint-smeared stain rubbed with charcoal.

What to do about the gift that's about to be taken away? What they gave us without asking for it, is snatched away – now that we were enjoying it – as if its intransigent owner were reclaiming it.

What should we do? Plead for postponements? Beg for crumbs of life which sooner or later will end up in the trash, in the garbage? Gorge oneself on the cure or in the search for other solutions offered by more or less mythical medicines? No. Man's only answer, the only one that can be measured with assurance against God's will, is to despise, to think of

---

* This statement, with all that implies religiously and metaphysically, deserves, at the very least, to be confronted with what other cosmogonies sustain: "Is it not time to create? The dawn of existence approaches. Whoever may aspire to life, be born! [...] The hour draws near, the hour of the one who aspires to birth, desiring it from Infinity." *(Popol Vuh)* (Author's Note)

that precious gift as something lacking transcendence, a mockery, like whatever comes and goes. With no other form of evaluation.

There also remains – it goes without saying – another solution: to precipitate the restitution of life, to select the place and the way to return it without any thanks, without any drama whatsoever.

*

The body becomes an object that demands every attention possible: a pitiless, intimate enemy that imposes a life sentence for the least distraction, the most fleeting deviation.

As day breaks the cures commence, in an inflexible though arbitrary order, advancing from head to toe, or vice-versa.

On one's rotten nails, on the leprous sole of the feet, between the toes where a whitish fungus, crafty and microscopic, takes root, then explodes into oozing boils and rashes, an oily, rancid antifungal ointment is applied. Then these feet must be wrapped in gauze bands fastened with rags until they look like mummies or medieval infants wrapped and camphorized against the Bubonic plague.

On one's knee: a rough-edged hole with a yellowish inside, a skin crater drowned by cortisone lotions, or thatched with antibiotic patches.

A greenish hyaline preparation – with a nauseating mentholated smell – is applied upon a persistent laceration, between the deflated gray-haired left testicle and the wrinkled diminished sex organ totally lacking in vigor.

Boringly simple exercises to increase breathing capacity.

A bowl of pills to swallow thinking of something else.

The gums and the tongue, with cotton and a toothpick, are moistened with a burning disinfectant liquid, to dissuade the disease from all possible intimidating advances.

Fortunately, at the moment, there's nothing on the head...

So here's the daily "menu": Fongamil on the feet and between the toes, and Diprosone on the sole of the foot; on the knee, penicillin; on the testicle, Borysterol.

The different bowls – on one of them there's a seascape, perhaps tropical, which decorates the bowl and distracts one from its content – hold Visken, Nepressol, Depakine, Malocide, Adiazine, Lederfoline, Retrovir (AZT) or in its place Videx (DDI), Immovane. The last one is only a sleeping pill. Also Cortancyl – before breakfast –, Zovirax, Diffuk and if necessary, Atarax.

Teldane, an allergy pill, Doliprane, for aches and pains, and Motilium, for nausea, are optional.

Once a month a tall skinny redhead makes his rounds, always in a short-sleeved shirt and a knitted tie. He carries as best he can a heavy dark cube-shaped machine that looks like a storage battery and which he immediately plugs in.

Through a plastic funnel that curls around itself like a compact trombone, the infected man inhales an antibiotic vapor that will protect him until the next visit, from all pulmonary infections.

When the inhalation is finished – it takes twenty minutes – the hospital nurse uncurls the funnel, wraps it carefully in paper and throws it into the garbage bag that someone will remove tomorrow.

Then the interrogation begins: "Did you feel nauseous, a choking sensation, a bitter taste in your mouth? Have they taken you, in the course of the month, to another hospital? Fever, sputum, dizziness?"

He gathers and straightens out his printed forms scribbled with no. He organizes them scrupulously in a small, wrinkled black valise. He notes down the next date and appointment hour, as if the hospice were overflowing with worldly activities and on the agenda of each inmate there were no room for further appointments.

He bends over to look at the books on the night table. Then I notice that he's wearing a beeper on his belt: at any moment he can receive an urgent call. He picks up a heavy volume of *Complete Works*.

He carefully sets down the volume: he livens up and remarks to me that he is reading something *very instructive* about the evolution of the species, in which it is demonstrated in an *incontestable fashion* that Darwin was wrong. Man – he adds – does not descend from the ape, but is rather something like his first cousin. They've proven this with eyeteeth and jawbones. And neither will he be the last link of the chain: we will be diminished and bald, like standing lizards. Science, he concludes, is wrong...

"It's true," I answer him testily, thinking about the chatterboxes who run this place more than about what he's saying, "but it would be futile at this point to resort to other systems, as natural as they might seem. Even if they come from the Orient. They only contribute to the general confusion."

He looks at me somewhat skeptically. He says good-bye respectfully, and leaves:

"See you next time!"

*

I'm well aware of it: they hate my voice. They barely conceal this. When they hear it, they shudder, as if they were hearing the squeaking of chalk against a dry blackboard, a squawk, a grinding of teeth.

I can't fix it, nor do I try: the voice is the body's truth, a merciless though immaterial witness, always another's.

As a young man, when I'd fall in love, my tone of voice would change. Absorbing passion, burning passion, both have abandoned me: what I now hear when I speak is a nasal echo, a grainy wrinkledness, which preceded the loss of energy and was like a herald of weakness.

The voice expires before the person and remains afterwards. Not its physical texture, which decays, breaks and falls, but rather its mental image, close to speech, which rises, as if drawn by the zenith of an invisible sun.

*

Before, I enjoyed a persistent illusion: I was one. Now we are two, inseparable, identical: the disease and me.

It seems that pregnancy produces the same sensation.

*

What hustle and bustle! If you didn't know what this was you'd think it was a luxury hotel, they all pass so often and quickly: tidy floor cleaners – insulting those who dare to walk on the wet surface –, servants bearing transparent jars, kitchen boys in their starched caps, and laundresses with piles of freshly ironed towels smelling of bleach and lavender.

Something, however, mockingly contradicts this euphoric image: the old women, in threadbare plush bathrobes and slippers, their coiffures in disarray, coming and going as they talk to themselves and gesticulate, like madwomen.

An old man unbuttons his coat and urinates right in the corridor.

*

"It can be stated, in fact, that Saint John of the Cross provides the elements for a *critique of the mystical Experience*. And that experience, according to his outline, *implies a negation of all appearances. All phenomena are rejected.* Mystical Experience cannot be the experience of an object, in the realist sense of the word. Neither is it the proof of a presence – since all feelings of presence are, still, a phenomenon.

"Mystical Experience is then, for Saint John of the Cross, something that transcends phenomena, whatever they may be. And we can only be certain of the divine when our forms of representation lack validity. There is no contradiction here: he is not the same I who, at first indecisive or defiant, later identifies with a God he declares his own.

"Saint John summarizes in the word *night* the nature of that experience. The negation of diverse objects, whether these be natural or supernatural, suggests to us what neither our senses nor our mental capacity could understand."

JEAN BARUZI, *L'intelligence mystique*

I lost. I bet on the human being. I thought that in him there was a part of God.

Today I find myself sick and alone.

At least one thing certain remains from all this: disillusionment.

*

They've brought the daughter of the redheaded woman. Identical to her mother, or to what her mother must have been forty years ago: the same tangles of singed hair, the same stiff manikin posture, also the same garments: bows, ringlets and flowery patterns everywhere. Very shiny eyes, like a harpy's. Surely the Cuban witchdoctor and the vampire are the ones who invited her. But, where is the old bag? Haven't seen her around.

*

Light on the continent opens what we perceive toward what we cannot see and what we cannot see follows immediately: it is here, all around, ever closer and ever more fleeting. Light which exposes the earth's continuity and leads us toward its time without end.

Island light, on the other hand, encloses: it falls here like lead, outlines off in a distance a precise surface – a rock that rises alone in the sea – and, with a double stroke, locks in isolation. A double light over the sea: a diffuse vapor in which clarity is erased, entered by the water before having touched it; sometimes, however, its brilliance is unbearable, like a mirror.

Here, on the islands, in the heart of these oceanic variations, there is no place for imprecision: everything is crystal clear, relentlessly precise, underlined; each thing is, first of all, the island in itself and, in an urgent way, what the island is.

Here life is something precise, surrounded by – one is not sure – either the vertigo of a mystery or the brutality of something impossible.

The island's present is what ceases; its future oscillates between myth and fatality.

*

Take a deep breath of sea air, tear the malady from the body, uproot it like a second untouchable and carbonic body that mixes with ours, overflowing it slightly like a lethal halo. Recover clarity, lightness.

Faraway, the limy white mountain of quartz, mica and plaster, with different green tints, divided in triangles by the morning shadows.

Sun. Solitude. Silence.

Behind appearances – persons and things – there is nothing. Neither is there any substance whatsoever behind images, whether they be material or mental. When the questions have dissolved – either before or after death – there are no answers. The origin of the universe, the reality of the subject, space and time and reincarnation appear then as obligatory "figures" of mental rhetoric.

*

My hands tremble. When I write, and whatever position I assume, the letters are squirmy scribbles. When I try to drink, the cup jingles. I can't eat anything that has to be balanced on a fork: victims of my trembling, the grains of rice fall on the table.

My gums bleed.

*

"I see them, those obstinate old men and women, yesteryear's multitude. Lame, heads dislocated, drooling, paralytic, senile, shoulders bending toward the grave, befuddled twanging tongues, hands twisted like exposed roots, ossified, deaf, stained with urine and fecal matter... I see them, glance over them one by one in the corners of the hospice, in their last refuge, their eyes shining with a suspicious tenderness.

"They feed them in bed, seated amidst large pillows, their knees at the height of their mouths, the feeding bowl bent toward them from above, balanced, so they can plunge the food into their gullet. They're showered with insults, but they're happy. They have a house, they have within reach the objects that make them feel like human beings, the voices they know, the communal broth, the bench, the rosary, the urinal. They are detested but feel good in the heat of that hatred. They recognize themselves in the sun and the wind, in the rain and the mud, in the remarks, the gossip, the scandals, in all that prolongs and sustains them: guarantee of their status of being alive. Here they are. They exist. With a confirmed, patented existence. Condemned but attached to things."

VERGILIO FERREIRA, Em nome da terra, 1990

*

The body need only liberate itself from social protocol to manifest its true nature: a bag of farts and excrement. A trash heap.

≈ 16

DEATH OF THE ARCHITECT

What if we changed the background? What if this topsy-turvy tale unfolded in a different place than the sanitized hospital, outside those walls of compulsive seagulls over the waves? One drowns in that world of anemia, of foul smells and enclosure, in which each character follows an irreversible decline into his emaciation, into his final loss of flesh: the disease atrophies and dries the muscles, which fall from the bones, like rags.

But, how to get out of here, how to escape the furious fondling of the devilish Mephistophelian twins?

I can't get Immortelle out, since, as you've seen, she has a screw loose. Right now all she does is pedal away on an orthopedic bicycle she bartered from a cripple – aided by the sinister gypsies who rule over such traffic – to lose a few extra pounds that blemish – she says, soaked in sweat – the shape of her hips.

For this intramural exercise, this suffering in place, she's put on an exaggeratedly cone-shaped black latex cap, like a paper peanut cone, and a panties and undershirt outfit of the same material.

As she pedals she imagines biking over a flowery road, without pebbles or cracks, amid glimmering calm lakes. On the horizon, rearing like the knight's steed in a chess piece – diurnal ivory – awaited the spirited chestnut-colored stallion.

"That guy is completely deaf," murmured Immortelle, incredulously wagging her head, which already shook on its own. "Completely deaf..."

"Who?"

It was Exile, who passed by distributing rustic homemade aspirin tablets that had to be broken into four pieces before you could swallow them.

"He who should listen to everything!" replied the energetic cyclist. And she accelerated vehemently.

Exile covered her mouth, to hide a big laugh.

"Look at me now," Immortelle complained: "swimming on dry land. Why don't they let me out a little, to explore those arid places and breath the saltpeter in the air? I'd like to see the ocean."

"Madam" concluded Exile, dryly; "can't you see that it's raining cats and dogs?" and she turned her back on her.

Immortelle suddenly stopped her hectic athletic activity. She remained in silence, motionless, crestfallen, as if toppling over herself, incapable of a monosyllable, of the slightest gesture. Her eyelids turned into purple stains; her nose, two leprous holes; her mouth, a twisted piggy bank slot.

She abandoned the bicycle and fell upon the *récamier*: her head and her feet flopped from one side to the other. She spent a whole day and night like this.

The next morning the watchman of the pentagon showed up smashed, having attenuated the austerity of his shift in the turbulent gas station cantinas along the highway.

He thought she was dead. He shook her hard, as if to bring back to life a drowned person, or a rag doll to breathe life into her:

"Señora, how are you?" and he continued to shake her.

She only muttered:

"The architect has died."

It was true. A brutal accident had carried off the sculptor, taking from the island the one who lived in its volcanic bowels and formed part of its lava.

Now the precursor rests in that black sand with which he sealed his respect for nature, in that rocky and arid ground he loved so much. The archipelago's lunar silence now envelops and protects him.

The abrupt night of the islands passes weightlessly over his stone garden.

She sank into another world – of lizards and sand, of swift little animals and porous, eyeless faces – a world of dementia.

17

IS THE BLUE BUGATTI READY YET?

Duty triumphed.

Help and Mercy, though pious, were efficient, and they picked up the panting, sad-looking creatures drenched in a fresh scarlet red fluid fast becoming rupestrian clots.

Mercy lifted the Horse, his eyes crossed and sparkling as if they were glass, his face wooden. He was a bloodied Sevillian Christ and the men had hoisted him to their shoulders to take him out for a parade. He heard the cheers, smelled the aroma of the candles and the fresh flowers wilting nearby; his naked torso had been scourged; a thick flap of black velvet with silver bows hung from his waist.

He fell again.

Once more, the stout fateful sister lifted him up.

"Now," she teased, "if we believed in the stinky medical marvels spread by these two, we would limit ourselves to a poultice of balsamic herbs, a spider web compress, or some nauseating concoction. Fortunately, other more realistic souls invented the suture! Annoyed, she ran to the medicine cabinet next door in search of a needle and thread. "Now we'll see what stayed with me after reading all those dressmaking magazines!"

The other nurse of that ferocious pair took care of Cayman. The saurian was writhing and weeping quietly like a poor lizard sprinkled with brine. While they searched for a more suitable practitioner, they wrapped Cayman's neck in strips of adhesive tape, then stretched and secured it in a humiliating ostrich position.

"And what do we do with them now?" inquired one of the sisters.

"The worst thing that could befall them..." replied the other without hesitation, thus carelessly allowing her true nature to surface. And she haughtily tossed back a lock of hair.

"Lavages with giant tubes?"

"Ay, my dear, you're too kind. The worst would be fresh orange juice."

"Orange juice?"

"Of course. But served at the same time and in the same dingy little room, so they'd have to put up with each other."

Of their purposes in life – to distinguish themselves from each other and to devote themselves solely to good – the albino twins, albeit barely, had accomplished the first.

Mercury, thanks to tortuous surgical manipulations – procured by God knows what defloration – now looked slant-eyed, Chinese white, a pearly glint on her cheeks and her jet hair gathered in three twists in a bun at the nape of her neck, so that the only thing missing was an ivory hairpin. She had assumed a dainty little laugh in place of the vulgar guffaws of yesteryear, making her seem like a silly nun of decidedly Eastern origins.

She had also changed her name, radically. To the extent that if anyone called her by her old names, she refused to respond, and she felt insulted if someone did not know or simply ignored this irreversible onomastic revolution. Never again would she be Mercy or Auxilio; from now on she would be Exilio AKA Exile.

"And me," argued Help when she suddenly learned of that switch, "I'm to be called neither Help nor Socorro but Cascorro? She shook the lacquered lock covering her right eye, tossing it aside only to say "Never!" She was the platinum blonde, black-eyed evil officer from the early talking films: the ideal muse for

Art Deco tubercular poets. Everyone found her very enigmatic. To tell the truth: she looked like living death.

As for Immortelle, you have to admit: she was like new. Nowadays she was a total woman, all svelte and spruced up, and standing tall as if she were wearing high spiked heels, with her thin arms, and long skinny hands. Not bad. Not bad at all. Especially if you recall that it was all the result of herbs, a phytotherapeutic achievement.

"Or a miracle of regression," and in harmonious ellipses she moved her arms, her sparkling purple nails.

She listened to everything with the elegance of those whose ears are plugged with wax. In profile? A bit stooped: her neck held straight by necklaces, like a lucumí deity, in order to hide the wrinkles. Her clothes? We won't mention them: every day more electric blue and more silver. The make-up, that was always pale, decidedly. Not from discretion; it was the fashion.

But the more the body of that spirited gal was regenerated and rejuvenated, the more the poor thing's mind deteriorated, as if the wonders worked by the beneficent brews were only skin deep, as if the stretching progressed in concert with senility and dementia.

Physically, she was good looking and alert; she spoke insightfully about the most complicated topics, appropriately combined proper names, remembered kingdoms and dates in order, but deep down inside she was losing her foothold, two or three tenacious songs, refrains from her childhood – the most stupid –, were taking over her mind; she conversed with the dead; she thought that she was at a worldly cocktail party after a geometric fashion show, and she'd throw back her head and roar with laughter at oft-repeated, worn-out jokes; she called to mind distant events in excessive, almost demonic detail, but she was incapable of remembering what happened yesterday.

She was ardent, it's true – old age is cold.

She was a doddering young woman.

One day she picked up a horrendous cross-eyed rubber doll that the prophetic sisters had brought her from a medical excursion and began to rock it, begging for warm milk for her baby. Holding him in her arms, she circled around the room, like an animal caged with its offspring.

That morning, as soon as she awoke, she ran to her dressing table to doll herself up. She didn't even take time to pee. The orientalized twin had messed up the three mirrors with adhesive tape, so that Immortelle saw herself topsy-turvy in a quicksilver puzzle, like a horde of harpies scratching their feathers.

Despite her recent stretching, she continued to visualize her body as an old lady's, crucified with wrinkles. Incapable of assimilating her new image, she applied layer upon layer of concoctions in hopes of making her skin smooth, which it mostly was already.

She longed – it goes without saying – for Cayman's morning potions, and wondered what might have become of him? Could the wicked sisters have turned him over to the authorities? And Horse, in what other pastures of pleasure might he be grazing, and with whom? But her mind scattered immediately amid other inquiries: for example, what she would wear this winter?

That day she was plastered with more cosmetics than a baroque mask for a municipal funeral celebration. She dressed in Prussian blue and donned a cute little silver hat that resembled a thimble. At ten A.M. she was sitting on the *récamier*, stiff and demure as if she were awaiting the verdict of a severe haute couture jury.

At twelve, when they brought her lunch – the usual damaged tomatoes and dry meat on stainless steel trays – they found her talking to herself. She was calmly arguing with someone – the nurse thought she heard – about the price of the embroidery on some firm tight-fitting tablecloths to be placed to rest on a balcony....

"So young and so delirious," the attendant lamented with a pious and mocking tone.

When, at three P.M. they came to pick up the trays, they found them untouched and Immortelle as dressed up and ready as before. But there was a change: the slow monologue had become a strident shouting, moving from a whispered *sotto voce* to a furious *fortissimo*, with backstitches of atonal crowing.

At four P.M. they had to inject her with a sedative.

It was useless.

Half an hour later and for the first time since she'd entered the hospice, she opened the door to her cave.

She looked at the white corridor in surprise, as if to ask where she was, what she was doing there, and even, perhaps, who she was.

For an instant she reflected. She ran along the corridor, toward the glass dome.

"The Bugatti," she shouted. "Is the blue Bugatti ready yet?"

They recovered her in a ravine near the pentagon. In a daze she had rolled over stones and pebbles; she was battered and blemished from the brambles, but even so she clung to her mad soliloquy with the fierce indifference to everything outside delirium – including her own body – and the ardent conviction that marks the discourse of all orators.

"Immortelle! Immortelle!" shouted the valiant saviors who had examined the surroundings of the colonial mansion stone by stone with giant lanterns.

From below she watched their black silhouettes standing out starkly on a background of reddish planets, probable angels and a shower of stars. The cone of light from the lanterns yellowed the rocks and grotesquely enlarged the bodies of the devoted rescue workers.

Amidst the bramble bushes the sisters grew in stature, reaching toward the sky until they ended in a tiny, moving tuft that seemed – like the heads of the possessed – to revolve on itself.

"Immortelle!" The two skinnies shouted in unison with their moist little voices. "We've come to save you!"

She straightened up, damaged but regal:

"Identical twins!" she shouted insultingly. And, with fierce conviction: "My name is Sonia!"

∽ 18

ORANGE JUICE TASTES SO DIVINE!

They – who else but the Horse and Cayman – had to gulp down their orange juice, together, on their rickety beds, entangled in their mended sheets – all this plotted perfidiously by the heteromorphic twins.

Of course the luxuriant salamanders, always on the lookout to do any supplementary good, had seasoned the juice with a potent hallucinogenic destined, Exile murmured with a grimace of fear, to provoke edenic visions with thousands of colors and little lights, which would remove their desire – an unpleasant testicular aftertaste, if there is such a thing – to boast and fight.

So they swallowed the cocktails and licked their lips with delight. Rolling his eyes, the Horse exclaimed:

"Orange juice tastes so divine!"

Cayman, erudite and Cuban, shot him an arrogant physician's glance while *in his mind* he reviewed the salutary properties of ascorbic acid, vulgarly known as vitamin C.

The Horse stood up. He remained erect with exceptional firmness, as if magnetized by the ground; his balance, more than simple stability, was the tension of a warrior ready for combat: muscles glued to his sides, fists clenched, his gaze defiant and angry. His body sculpted in one piece from the trunk of an acana tree.

Shooting out from him came hooves that pounded the linoleum, followed by horseshoes so heavy they seemed like mortars, filled with nails and in the center, a spike. He sprouted wings with three rows of different feathers, and upon them a peacock's eyes and iridescence. His skin: shining tanned leather, muscles of flexible steel. Attached to his tail was a slender mask, like half a melon, with globular eyes and a very long nose. Springing from his head were two delicate, curved ivory horns like seals' fangs, but unlike those of unicorns, which bend forward, his bent backwards. He was trailed by a merry little circular face with a long tail of black worsted yarn.

He neighed.

He tossed his mane.

He unfurled his wings.

He took off.

He passed, as in slow motion, through the window into the transparency of night. Cayman saw him way up in the sky, armed with stars, like the drawings done by children who outline a figure by connecting numbers. Above the archipelago he was an immense constellation.

A sign of something.

Or rather, since lysergic hallucinations coexist and can easily overlap, Cayman perceived him quite differently on another day, under the wildly lecherous influence of the potion.

He was now nothing less than a tall, very fine-featured damsel with blue eyes and an aquiline nose. Her long black hair cascaded to her shoulders. Covering her was a crackly sparkling red blanket woven with flaming flamboyant flowers; she was crowned with a gold tiara studded with pearls and heavy rubies. Her necklaces were so numerous and so resonant that when she stroked them she was enveloped in fragile music of miniscule maracas, or of sand coursing through an empty bamboo stalk: they were beads alternately matte white and burgundy red.

But most surprising were her attributes: in her left hand she brandished a shining carved silver chalice and in her right a sword. A halo of light, like tiny trembling flames, irradiated from her body.

Red apples appeared around her swift feet. The bittersweet aroma of the fruit invaded the room and the entire hospital, so much so that all those enervated souls enjoying the Mediterranean sun beneath the pentagonal dome thought that someone was preparing them an exquisite applesauce caramelized with brown sugar.

A violent flash of lightening zebrined the sky.

It was that smell of apples, so characteristic of sweet medicine – the traditional pharmacists were reclaiming the hospital, with their retinue of tourniquets and scalpels, injections and punctures – that made Immortelle believe that the two animals weren't far off. She decided to look for them, certain that the three of them together would be clever enough to break out of the sinister hospital.

So, like a bloodhound sniffing the underground trail of a mole, the intrepid redhead traversed the five converging arabesque-festooned corridors beneath the glass dome. One by one, she pushed open the doors, finding each time a sort of macabre theater, with its adhesive tape stage machinery, its orthopedic props and its livid or yellowish gesticulating exhausted protagonists who looked as though their faces had been smeared with chalk dust or saffron.

Until at the end of the corridor where kitchens alternated with urology labs – would they use the same containers? – she came upon the cage that – she supposed – had housed the two dull-skinned wild beasts.

Only the smell of apples lingered.

They had been there, for sure: strewn on their rickety beds, as in the sudden getaway of a male nurse, were soiled housecoats and green nylon caps and gloves. Also, on the floor there were some large red leather slippers that she recognized immediately.

Not the least doubt: they'd jumped out the window – which, however, represented no great effort on their part – and escaped perhaps forever, who knows why.

She looked calmly at all the objects and at what there was between them, as if the emptiness were something tactile, material.

You could still perceive the din of their flight, a trace stored in the air, an inaudible echo of a mortal leap.

She closed the door carefully, as if she wanted to preserve the inner silence or respect the delicate dream of a convalescent.

And she returned to the *suite impériale*.

She picked up the miniaturized cat asleep on the *récamier*, and gave him a kiss. His nose was cold.

Grabbing an issue of *Harper's Bazaar*, she glanced through it and placed it back on the pile.

She put on the most luxurious garment she could find in her trunk, looking in the multiple mirror at the way the pleats fell.

She returned, this time on tiptoe, to the corridor with labs and kitchens. She unbolted the door at the end.

Before leaving, she looked in the opposite direction for the last time at the bluish light filtering through the glass dome.

19

UNDER THE LINDEN TREES

"Two scoundrels. That's what they were."

"No; they wanted to heal."

"If that were the case, why did they disappear?"

"They didn't take anything."

"Or leave anything."

Throughout the interminable day the recluses gathered under the linden trees, in the island's burning summer. They were seeking some lighter air, the calm that emanates from new leaves, eager – with the excess demanded of all compensations – for their last remaining pleasure: silent, complicit company, or abrupt, muddled conversation.

"Fear, from morning to night, prevailed. Fear of contagion, of weakness. But they still carried it within."

The stony path from the hospice to the trees exhausted them. They arrived out of breath and enervated and dropped onto the iron benches that the gypsies had taken from the pentagon. Immediately they opened the woven dried palm leaf pouches they had brought with them, and without making a toast, they devoured small loaves of raisin bread and soft drinks, pressing their beggar's bags against their chests, as if afraid of theft.

"The rejuvenated redhead wasn't sick. Nor is she. Crazy, that's what she was."

"They frequented someone else, a woman who really was young."

"That's impossible. They certainly knew about the risk of contagion."

"Yes. But they were driven by something unappeasable: the flip side of everything medical, the other face of benefactors and saints, the attraction of slime, the delight of corruption. To sink all the way to the purulent, in order to rise then to immaterial light."

The reverberation from the hospice was so great that they saw the branches of the trees as orthogonal gray lines and their foliage as masses of different greens. Narcotized by the lethargic virtues of linden, the old men fell into a bottomless siesta, as into a trance.

"They'll be back."

"Yes, but sick, like everyone else. To see their own bodies from without, like objects for experimentation, while the malady carries out its patient work. They'll apply to themselves what they learned from us."

The few trees were again green. Their branches reappeared. The fresh, yellow tops vibrant with little leaves rose as if they wanted to unite heaven and earth in the motionless time of the vegetal kingdom.

One day, around the group fluttered a butterfly of such intense blue—oceanic turquoise, cobalt from an African migration—that they sat in silence, mute from the violence of that color.

A battery-operated radio loaned to them by an attendant—they hummed tunes from long ago—, a round of lemonade, fresh news from the Continent, and even the furtive step of an evangelical pastor lost in those parts and suffocating from the heat: such were the opaque miracles that brightened their endless days until, very late, the sun would set.

Fodder for the implacable devouring of forgetfulness: an hour later the melodies of yore had faded, the lemonade had grown warm, the pastor's threatening message and the news had intermingled and become gobbledy-gook.

Everything was resplendent, instantaneous. Ungraspable, like color.

Or, rather, what memory preserved was like a deformed double of people and things, but not at all revelatory. A uselessly avaricious stockpile. So that of the Horse remained neither the treatments, nor his inopportune guffaws in the silence imposed by the hospital, nor his large slippers, nor the ax of his huge front teeth – only the strange grammatical mistakes he made when he spoke, shuffling verbal declensions according to his whims.

To that bric-à-brac of memories, Cayman willed only his well-filed nails and – more significant – his madman's gaze.

Nothing marked them definitively, not even horror.

"To survive. Day after day."

"I'm happy to die. As soon as possible."

So as not to witness the hecatomb suffered by the survivors.

"And her? What will be left to us of her?"

"A streak of henna when she'd toss her hair in the shadows. The red of those copper strands. Nothing more."

"Yes. Something else will remain with us. Because in her the essential was the accessory, what for others was the forgettable detail: flashy rags, tarnished jewels, shoes, and hats. The sense of life as a fashion show."

A dress sparkles an instant and will immediately be useless, indistinct, even ridiculous. A castoff: like the body we surrender to death. Dresses, like butterflies, dazzle and fall. *La mode, c'est la mort.*

Suddenly, as always, the brief twilight of those islands fell.

Slow, unsteady, leaning on each other, they began their return to the pentagon.

They did not look, not even once, at the treetops.

They did not say good-bye.

20

TOWARD THE SEA

Amid pebbles, underbrush, stony paths, spiky flagstones and nettles the happy though battered fugitive made her way. She could finally practice the survivor's ten commandments taught her by Cayman – the physician had formulated them during his harsh Havana nights, which, it's true, had fostered even more murky fantasies.

It all helped one to float – the oxymoron is apropos – in this bare dry desert, to confront the open country and the blazing sun, obscured by sandy gusts of salty wind.

She was bewildered by such freedom; she took deep breaths of the pure, disinfectant-free, clean-smelling air; she sang to herself. But she was hungry and thirsty and afraid of what could happen to her – brigands, demons, wrong turns, storms – in those places without houses or trees to orient her.

She had avoided the paved road used by the ambulances to fool the proficiency of eventual pursuers.

At times she was consoled by minimal joys: on a sphere-shaped bush the size of a dark river dwarf, and completely bristling with thorns, she found succulent berries – pomegranate red, a cross between the raspberry and elderberry – that looked like jewels. She devoured them voraciously. Her hands were red from the violent pricks of the thorns and her mouth even redder, from the juice.

She ended up, besides, with spasmodic stomach cramps and waves of diarrhea that she had to pacify with rhizome antidotes, if she could find them.

And so she would lift her damask skirts – for that unprecedented pilgrimage she had dressed as a *fin de siècle* courtesan – and futilely fertilize the ungrateful earth.

When she reached the crossroads, which she'd so often passed in her youth, she realized that everything had changed.

It was twilight of the second day; the sun was setting toward the beach with a lavish display of pale pinks and threads of gold. Immortelle stopped for a moment under a signpost on the road, turned toward the sunset, and in silence contemplated the descent of the trembling copper disc.

On the arrows of the signpost the Indian names had been covered by names that corresponded to the founders' supposed implantations, covered again by the summer residences of collectors and archeologists, and finally replaced with names in another language that Immortelle could not even read.

She continued toward the sea, revived by a crust of bread and a bit of fresh water, offered to her by a ragged young beggar with penetrating eyes – surely a philosopher.

She went from one surprise to the next: dazed, mouth open, mute.

The gypsies' stand, where in former times there were only frolicking little brats and fat women with billowing silvery skirts and a pail of water on their heads, was now bedecked with an orange hollyhock fresco, a screeching irreverence to the twilight, and a flamenco dancer, fisherman or bullfighter on which a streetlamp cast light and shadow. From two loudspeakers emanated a repulsive melody of ostensibly Andalusian origin, which one would learn by heart, replacing an equally dumb tune from the year before.

Lime plaster walls. Wrought iron windows. Two cars at the door. The former charterhouse, so restored it looked like a maquette, or a new building constructed with graftings from ruins, was actually only a parenthesis between two blue-tiled Olympic pools with nickel-plated steps and two diving boards. A fragile, fussy little garden connected a harsh exterior to that laborious exercise in postmodern architecture which, in turn, led to a glass pyramid near the road – rhombuses assembled with chrome ribbing – of uncertain size and utility. A shiny dome wrought with similar craft and materials perched on the roof, opened in two halves like a grapefruit.

The head on tiptoes was still there, with the same cockatoo on its shoulder.

It was actually a little old man, wrinkled like a raisin. The tiny head that crowned him looked more like a copy of a head shrunken by the Guaitaca Indians than a human appendage. The little eyes were so lively and transparent that he seemed to smile with his gaze.

The cockatoo had seen better days, as was to be expected: it was craw and feather and little else, with four ashen tufts and such a bitter disposition that, whenever anyone came near, he'd begin hurling insults and pecking at the air.

Without further preamble, Immortelle implored him:

"I am seeking two men."

The pinhead opened his eyes very wide:

"What do they look like?"

"One looks like a horse; the other has eyes like an owl."

"Some time ago, they were at the house of the old woman with the doll. They buried her in the dovecote and threw corn on the ground. The doves died, as did lots of other birds. They piled them up in wooden boxes and threw them in the garbage."

"Faggot! Faggot!" the boorish old bird hurled a strident scream.

Immortelle hurried away, shocked by such disorder.

The hamlet was a mass of indistinguishable prefabricated houses, each endowed with a front garden with two dry square flowerbeds and a wagon wheel – the intentions were visibly bucolic – and, as a finishing touch, on the border, four opportune flowerpots.

Some people, out of tacky arrogance, had personalized that rectangular aridity with concrete fauns, huge earthen vats imported from Camaguey for an exorbitant sum, fountains of caracoling rococo in their most grotesque mother-of-pearl version, mermaids, and even Snow White's seven dwarves with their brick-red bonnets.

The streets met at a right angle. Closed doors and windows.

Now there were two gas stations, with their pump hoses and blackened-faced mechanics in blue overalls. Their advertisement was a seashell painted on a tin fence that rattled in the wind.

She left that limbo, always toward the sea.

She listened to the hum of the highway.

She could make out in the distance two giant blue flickering neon lights, so high that one could distinguish the figures they traced against the sky: a colossal lizard standing on its two hind legs, or rather a salamander; beside it, also in that improbable position, a bird. It was a snack bar.

A self-service.

A *fast food*.

A quartz platform shielded by a tall Plexiglas window. And a little stone garden.

The establishment's infrequent clients – as infrequent as the cars on the highway – greedily gobbled a transparent greenish jelly in plastic bowls that served as aperitif, first course, main course and dessert, agglutinated in trembling mounds, as if a seismic tremor were shaking the ground.

"The energetic properties of algae," explained an employee wearing a severe bonnet and thick glasses, while she seasoned a purée of the same consistency with sauce from a little packet, "are limitless."

Her argument soon seduced Immortelle, who choked on two spoonfuls of the extract:

"Delicious!" she noted. "Between the pork roast marinated with guava leaves and the Basque codfish stew, with a touch..." she recollected savoring it, with a blank stare, "of jerked beef... No: bacon."

"Besides," continued the courageous clerk, "this nectar will be our only food when they finish building the underwater cities between the islands."

"And air?" Immortelle inquired.

"Ay, señora: oxygen, like they do on the Moon."

It was a veritable feast of vital cream. Which left her stuffed and greenish.

"It's like devouring health," she concluded, elegantly dissembling a belch. "The sea is the origin..."

"And will be the end of everything," stressed the savvy girl. "There will be underwater crevasses and planetary tremors. The whales already detect them and that's why they're committing suicide. When they are kept damp with sponges so that their skin doesn't dry up, they look upon human beings with such sadness...."

The most noteworthy aspect of the place – which on the one hand was only a few cube-shaped tables with live lizards inside, and some chairs imitating orchids whose pistils were head phones, broadcasting tribal music – was the clothing worn by the customers, the last avatars of the naturists.

Black fiber pants, naked torsos. All faces painted with intimidating masks: Japanese, African, Peruvian devils from the high Andes, protective monsters from Tibet. Black stripes on their arms. Arm and wrist bracelets adorned with razor blades. Miniature forts of white feathers on their heads.

One of them, a chunky big-mouthed bossy type, wore a dark cloak, which floated as he passed and seemed lighter than air. Like bat wings.

Immortelle, with her iridescent taffeta skirt, her damask and gold laces, and her soft Art Nouveau hat, whence protruded four reddish locks – all dusty and disarranged after the long march –, seemed a typical *habituée* of the place.

She pretended not to be amazed.

She sank into the orchid and collapsed in exhaustion.

But the shock troops began to abandon the coast, the highway and the adjoining gasoline stations.

The insidious rumor had made its way to those parts about the existence of another jelly more tonic, more invigorating and more beneficial for erections – secreted by the industrious, golden, hardworking and nocturnal queen of the lunar bees. You had to reach the ridges inhabited by the astral worker bees.

You had to ascend on foot, for long days in the sun and the night air, as did the Tarahumara Indians in their search for mushrooms – a collective, impious calvary – to achieve access to the royal alchemy, to the sublimation of the sulphur-colored pollen, to that dimmed magnetism emanating from the satellite.

She rose to follow them. Move with them toward the future and go back in time with herself, with the lugubrious parcel of her body, forty years back.

But she reconsidered.

She no longer had the drive for such efforts. Old age returned, incurable, even more stealthily than the disease.

She left the self-service, moved slowly, but not toward the interior, rather toward the coast. She crossed the highway. From their immense trucks shining like mirrors, saturating the air as they passed with irritating nonsensical music, the drivers – naked torsos and caps on their heads – shouted obscenities at her. Because of her attire, perhaps, or because she was crossing like a sleepwalker, without looking both ways.

She reached the strip of reefs. Crossed it as well as she could, now breathing in the fresh smell of the calm gray sea, devoid of reflections.

Damp sand. Her footsteps remained for a moment, then the cool morning breeze erased them.

She encountered the fractured, funereal ruins of the underground house. The extinguished volcano was collapsing upon itself, like a meteor smashed to bits by its own impact.

She descended some of the basalt-sculpted steps. But she could penetrate the earth no further. Blocking her way, as if to mark a reconquered territory, were fiery lizards, and a fluttering of strident birds.

If she remained there, against wind and tide, if she returned to the hospice – how and with whom? –, if she again saw the saurian and the equine, if she continued to age or recuperated her twice-lost youth...

Connections and conclusions I will return to relate.

If Death, that bald woman, always ready to pounce, grants me a reprieve.

21

THE COSMOLOGIST'S DIARY

Old men
seated
together, very close
long abandoned corridor
low voices.
They barely notice
the imperial monument
when the light goes.

Thinning hair,
gray clothes,
they embrace
trembling with cold.
Now distant,
exiled from themselves,
memory
doubles detect each other.
Alert.

Red leather coat,
simple hat,
alone, she gestures;
opens her arms wide
welcomes
an invisible lover
who hurriedly returns.
The always-alien energy
of illumination or dementia
startles her.
Her hand open,
she refuses a gift,
smiles, argues, waves,
sketches a faint amazement.
She has resumed the dialogue
sustained one day
                with her mirror.

With viscera torn out,
with tongue protruding,
with lips painted
with brine.

With wounded eyelids,
with his sex studded,
a clot
        smeared on his face.

With a cross,
with a coin,
with the lines on his hand
sewn on his tongue.
With eyes covered,
with fingers sewn.
with feet lacerated.
With a word inscribed
in his wounded mouth:
with dark chalk.

With black semen,
with the eye rolled white,
one's bones in flame:
                insanity.

Close the shapes
And the walls, stone by stone,
to outside noise
then rest on them,
cloistered.
Like the echoes
of canticles
fading
in the silence,
                    the one.

II

She looked at her fingers,
something was raveling and unraveling
in the blue pick-up truck.
Detestable mania of cutting one's nails,
calculating one's taxes
or reading the news
at the door of the temple.
(From the bar across the street
you can hear the organ
when the rain stops.)

III

To the central void
the wheel
owes its motion;
to white
color
its brilliance.
Someone coughs during the prayer,
A bird flies by:

                  inconceivable silence.

HAPPINESS

In the country,
listening to the night rain,
the steady rain of autumn,
the wind from the coast always close.
Unable to move in bed:
prevented
            by two cats.

Throw off your clothes.
Rub alcohol on your hands.
Wash your hair.
Don't use perfume; hot water baths,
herbs.
Let no pore
smell
            of death.

I will open my eyes
To weightless light,
Unbounded day
devoid of beginning,
Stop thought,
Remove the image,
its brutal succession,
and even desire
– the last to depart,
the heir.
Hanging below
toward non-being,
where no divinity
appears
nor the least range of color.
Nor white.
Nor silence.

Close your eyes
to light, to every possible image.
Observe in silence
neither approving nor condemning
watch, as they disappear
agreements, memories,
mental representations,
darkness, affections.

Coarse emblem of the void,
remain in that fragile zero
– not even the sensing
another presence.

Learn not to be.
Merge with nonbeing. Go.

Thinking about something else
– a buried treasure – something I don't find
poppy after poppy
I've beheaded the whole garden.

And so, some dry summer afternoon
at the edge of the seeded rows
death, seemingly unthinking,
will sever a head – mine.

                    Marina Tsvetaeva
                    September 5–6, 1936

TRANSLATORS' AFTERWORD

In his lifetime Severo Sarduy (1937–1993) was best known for his exquisitely wrought neo-baroque prose, but he was also an abstract painter and his production includes plays and poetry in addition to fiction and essays. As a youth, he abandoned medical school for the world of art and literature, leaving his native Cuba shortly after the Revolution in 1960, initially on a scholarship from the Cuban government to study museum curatorship at the Louvre. Of that fateful year which determined the rest of his life, Sarduy remarked in an autobiographical sketch, with his customary wit:

> 1960 – Europe and/or the Louvre. All of Europe is a museum, just as all of Oklahoma is a theater for Kafka. Four years follow in which I take noses off sculptures and put them back on, and I finish writing a thesis on the Flavian emperors. From this comes one sentence in my literary works: Dolores Rondon's hairdo is that of Julia Titi, the emperor's daughter. I travel around Europe.[*]

Despite the fact that he did not return – and even became a French citizen – Sarduy is not usually pegged as a Cuban "exile" writer in the adverse political ways that affected the lives

---

[*] Severo Sarduy, "Chronology," tr. Suzanne Jill Levine, *Review 72* (New York: Center for Inter-American Relations, 1972), 26. Dolores Rondon is a colorful "character" in *From Cuba with a Song*.

and legacies of his contemporaries such as Guillermo Cabrera Infante and Reinaldo Arenas. This circumstance, along with the complex nature of his writing, his close association with the Parisian literary scene of the 1960s and 1970s, and his markedly gay Cuban sensibility have made him hard to place for non-Cuban readers, especially during the years when Latin American "Boom" writers like Gabriel García Márquez were being introduced and translated into English. Living in Paris and being aligned, as Sarduy was, with the experimentations of the well-known Tel Quel group and with intellectuals such as Lacan and Barthes, who were his personal friends, the commentary on Cuba and colonialism found in Sarduy's books has seemed foreign to the image of Latin American literature formed by critical discourse and translation.

New York writer Bruce Benderson aptly described Sarduy's foreignness, after reading *Cobra* in English in 1975:

> I hacked my way through a text I can only describe as "tropical" – overfoliated, procreative, and intricate. But by tropical I also mean – ever vigilant, unblinking like the sun; for, to keep from going mad from the heat, tropical writing is always rigorously structured. Behind the riot of Sarduy's fiestas are months of grueling rehearsal. Severo Sarduy was a baroque comedian and a callused workhorse in one....Each jewel-like sentence is structured with tawdry detail, only to unfold like a paper origami trick into a new and more convoluted gesticulation, a new sacrilege.[*]

Benderson's comments refer to Sarduy's perhaps most celebrated novel, but they could easily describe his work as a whole, in particular the challenge which it presents to the reader. Flamboyantly gay in his ornate Cuban way, his writing dazzling but defiantly difficult, Sarduy was in a class by

---

[*] Bruce Benderson, "Tel Quel's Gaudy Harlequin." *Lambda Book Report* 4.11, July/August 1995, 17. Cited with the kind permission of the author.

himself. This has meant that his readership has been limited; however, it has meant as well that he has consistently enjoyed a select but highly devoted following in Spanish and also in translation. In English, for example, translations have been published of his novels (*From Cuba with a Song*, *Cobra* and *Maitreya*), essays (*Written on a Body* and *Christ on the Rue Jacob*), and plays (*For Voice*), some of them in the early 1970s, and his work has been included in specialized anthologies (Gay/AIDS or *avant-garde* literature). Readers appreciate his ability to bring together the scriptural and the plastic in a way that constitutes a bold new perspective not only on creative practices but also on issues such as AIDS and homosexuality, thus offering a glimpse both experiential and theoretical of a radically "different" Latin America, one that has often been repressed in literature and in society as a whole.

Beach Birds (Pájaros de la playa), published in 1993 within a few months after Sarduy's death, is at once a moving and parodic, at times even a humorous mockery of human effort to counter death and physical decline. François Wahl, a French intellectual and publisher (of the distinguished press *Editions du Seuil* with which Sarduy would work many years as acquisition editor of Latin American literature) who befriended the young Cuban in 1960, explains that originally Sarduy had intended to write a novel titled *Caimán* (Cayman) which, along with *Colibrí* and *Cocuyo*, would form a trilogy.* However, while Sarduy was working on the first chapter, he learned of his illness and his plans for the book changed: "pájaros de la playa," the name he had assigned to the gymnasts in Chapter One, was used to refer to the group of patients gathered on the island and it also became the book's title. Typical of Sarduy's texts, the use of "beach birds" alludes both to "high art" (specifically the ballet conceived by Merce Cunningham in collaboration with

---

* François Wahl, "Severo de la Rue Jacob," Severo Sarduy, *Obra completa*, eds. Gustavo Guerrero and François Wahl, Madrid: ALLCA XX, 1999. vol. II, p. 1500.

John Cage who was one of several avant-garde artists admired by Sarduy) and to street culture, in this case, a common and derogatory Cuban term for "fag" being "pájaro" or "pato" – bird or duck.

The plot of the novel is not difficult to outline, even though the elusive writing itself is dense. On a colonial island that at one time was a retreat for nudist athletes and is now filled with disease-infested birds, a large, crumbling mansion serves as a refuge and hospital for young men prematurely withered by illness. The name of their illness is never stated, although its resemblance to AIDS is clear, particularly in light of Sarduy's earlier work – especially the essays in *Christ on the Rue Jacob* – and his physical condition while he was writing the novel. Indeed, much in the same way that Sarduy must have suffered pain and discouragement – yet never abandoning his sense of humor, perhaps defiantly – as he worked on *Pájaros de la playa*, one of the central characters in the book and the narrator of some of the novel's most significant sections is a wheelchair-bound, paralytic patient at the hospital. His illness is nearing the final stages, his voice is barely audible, and one might expect his spirit to succumb to despair and the novel to be a tale of unremitting grief. This, however, is not what happens. The presence and perspectives of other more farcical characters – such as Immortelle, who is not ill but is desperately searching for the youth she is destined not to find, and Horse and Cayman, her two (rival) physicians – mockingly subvert the narrative with their antics, bizarre medications, and extreme diets. In addition, the wheel chair bound patient (known as the Cosmologist) records a gradual movement towards a certain clarity, an apprenticeship of "learning not to be."

As in Sarduy's previous work, the age-old dance of life and death is a dance in which everyone must participate. In this book, though, the narrator suggests that one can live through that dance, not in the sense of outwitting death – which, inevitably, none of the characters is able to do – but in the sense that an awareness of continual death, as a process inseparable from continual life, can allow one to be inspired by the dance. One can then enter it either with playfulness and parody and/ or train oneself to experience a state of non-being that will continue even when the body no longer dances. In Sarduy's case, that non-being is bound inextricably to the formal, elaborately crafted fictional world he created through the complex re-presentation of other fictions and by whose aesthetics he both lived and died as he wrote *Pájaros de la playa*.*

One of those other fictional worlds to which Sarduy returns in *Pájaros de la* playa is his early novel *From Cuba with a Song*, perhaps to suggest that the generic desert island in his last novel is Cuba as well as other islands, real and allegorical. Among the allegories stands out, of course, the Island of the Dead – a mythical and pictorial *topos* – here, a possible allusion to the very real "sidatorios" or AIDS colonies where Castro's government interned HIV patients to prevent contagion on the rest of the island.† Other "real" islands in Sarduy's mobile life include Sri Lanka (then Ceylon), and most specifically, volcanic

---

* In an interview with Jorge Schwartz ("Con Severo en Río de Janeiro, *Obra completa*, vol. II, p. 1834), Sarduy stressed the importance of adhering to the Buddhist way of life, which required (and, implicitly enabled) him to live "in harmony, emanate a truth, a knowledge – that of his writing, his text" (a text, it is important to note) that was always – as Sarduy made clear, the function of an artificial code selected to tell his story and to which he clung, "as if it were a life preserver" (interview with Gustavo Guerrero, "Reflexión, ampliación, cámara de eco: Entrevista con Severo Sarduy," Severo Sarduy, *Obra completa..* vol. II, p. 1835.)

† Although Sarduy probably did not have Manhattan in mind when he wrote *Pájaros de la playa*, a reader in English might well think of that island, on which, during the 1980s AIDS was experienced and discussed as a plague whose "dictatorial cruelty," in the words of Andrew Holleran, "touched ev-erything" ("Reading and Writing," *Ground Zero*, New York: Plume, 1988.) p. 2. How ironic, then, that Holleran uses the following quote to exemplify the attitude of those (non-homosexuals) who had no fear of becoming infected with the virus: "They should be put on an island and let 'em all die." (p.11). In this context it is also worth nothing that one of the characters in Holleran's novel *Grief* refers to the 1980s as a decade of "Funerals, funerals, funerals!" [of AIDS victims] (New York: Hyperion, 2006,) p. 50

Tenerife. Sarduy was often invited to lecture there, and he had a special affinity for the balmy Canary Islands: floating between Spain and the New World, these islands were the geographical origin of many Cuban families whose ancestors centuries ago boarded the Spanish galleons (stopping to pick up fresh supplies) to seek their fortune in the "Hispaniola" of Spain's imperial era. Indeed, Wahl explains that the island in Sarduy's last novel is a synthesis of Lanzarote and Tenerife, noting as well several additional references to these islands, in particular the house, person, and death of architect César Manrique.*

The reference to *From Cuba with a Song* also includes an affectionate return to a pair of characters: Auxilio and Socorro. Typical of Sarduy's characters (in Sarduy characters are more often than not hallucinatory doubles and metamorphic figures rather than psychological clones of real people) these two beings who resurface in *Pájaros de la playa* are comical twin helpers who recall Kafka's exasperatingly unhelpful and intrusive "assistants" in *The Castle*. Their names are exclamations, which translate in English as Help and Mercy. In our translation, this was one of many puzzles that needed solving: we played doubles to these doubles as we argued the pros and cons of repeating the translation of their names which Jill had chosen in *From Cuba with a Song* (1972), considering that the reader would not capture the humor of these names if they were left in Spanish. However, in *Pájaros de la playa* Sarduy uses Auxilio to evoke Exilio, exile – and Socorro to suggest Cascorro, a place in his native region of Cuba: for obvious reasons these were important references. We came to a "Sarduyian" solution, allowing the terms to produce offspring, as it were, in this case to echo each other in two languages (the added material appears in italics): "...Never again would she be *Mercy or* Auxilio; from now on she would be Exilio AKA *Exile.*

---

* Wahl, "Severo de la Rue Jacob," p. 1501

... "And me," argued Help.... "I'm to be called *neither Help nor Socorro* but Cascorro?" (ms. 128)

By "Sarduyian," as used above, we mean baroque, the tendency to proliferate synonyms or a chain of related signs, as it were, the search for a way to break through ambiguity and polyvalence toward signification(s). It is this tendency that might comprise the greatest challenge in translating Sarduy's work, for to translate Sarduy is to communicate the polyvalence of the playful and yet methodical poetics of allusive resonances and repetitions that characterized his writing from the beginning.

A notable example of this resonant repetition is the birds, not only as beach birds but also as the *palomas* that appear throughout the narrative. *Paloma* means both dove and pigeon in English, dove being a type of pigeon, so our quandary was: should we use one bird or the other, or both, or should we leave the Spanish (hence exoticizing) word *paloma* – which in English has other meanings not related to birds. Sometimes the novel's *palomas* seem more dove-like, symbolizing a sought-after peace, love and even purity, but other times they definitely appear to be ordinary urban pigeons, gathering en masse, flying ominously around the towers of the sanatorium, suggesting plague, infestation, contagion. There is even some talk of eating pigeon broth, which seems very un-dovelike, and indeed more squab-like, complicating the dilemma even further. These birds are more prominent in Chapter Five than in others, but we felt that it was important to be consistent, in order for the reader to recognize the repetition. We ultimately settled for the 'poetic' solution, populating the island of the dying with the white dove, and the text with its "d", its single syllable, its rhyme with "love" – its sound as significant as its sense.

The knotty polyvalence of the beach birds, however, is only one aspect of their role in the novel. Equally important, and this too was an issue for translation, is the intertextuality that links the birds – and thus the novel as a whole – with other literary works. As in the case of Help and Mercy, who introduce *From Cuba with a Song*, the birds call to mind Sarduy's earlier writing, in particular his untranslated novel *Colibrí* [Hummingbird] and perhaps most specifically, "El texto devorado" (The Devoured Text), an essay about Spanish novelist Juan Goytisolo's *Las virtudes del pájaro solitario* (*The Virtues of the Solitary Bird*) which Sarduy published shortly before he began *Pájaros de la playa*. In that essay, Sarduy discusses the rich complexity of Goytisolo's novel by commenting that in order to produce such a text its author must have devoured all the texts that preceded it, including his (Goytisolo's) own, thereby surpassing mere reading: he lived, incarnated or cannibalized, hence became those texts. Some of the texts that would have preceded Goytisolo's *Virtudes*, of course, relate to the solitary bird and its allusive presence in the book – where it is closely related to a "group of 'rare' birds" that includes the one in a lost work by Saint John of the Cross and those in *The Conference of the Birds*, a mystical poem by twelfth-century Persian author Farid ud-Din Attar.* Jorge Luis Borges, one of Sarduy's literary mentors, referred repeatedly to this Persian legend in his works as it preached most persuasively the Buddhist concept of God as No One or all of us, the "nothingness of personality," or plainly, the oneness of all humanity. In addition, since Goytisolo's novel "represents AIDS and how AIDS in representation, is received,"† the birds have (homo)sexual as well as mystical connotations. Sarduy makes this clear by closing his essay with an experience of his own in some Parisian baths, which he describes as both a Simorg – i.e., the name of the bird(s) in the legend, hence, metonymically, the gathering place for exotic mystical birds – and a Foucauldian "heterotopia" composed of disparate places.

---

* Bradley S. Epps, *Significant Violence: Oppression and Resistance in the Later Narrative of Juan Goytisolo* (Oxford: Oxford University Press, 1996). p. 380

† *Ibid.*

However, the passage in "El texto devorado" that is undoubtedly the most arresting with respect to *Pájaros de la playa* is the passage in which Sarduy describes the upper floor of the baths where one could see *palomas*, poisoned by smog, smash against a skylight directly overhead. Reading that passage, one cannot but think of the strikingly similar passage in *Pájaros de la playa* (Chapter Two), in which a gale-force wind shatters the glass in the cupola and a (solitary) heron lands on the window of the bewildered blonde. The heron has apparently consumed some lethal substance and, in a way reminiscent of Sarduy's discussion of Goytisolo, whose hand had exuded – vomited – the devoured texts, the heron vomits the substance it has ingested and then succumbs. Sarduy comments that from the memorable afternoons he spent in those baths what remains is *Colibrí*, a "forgettable book" from the same quill as "this solitary bird."

The importance of the co-incidence of these passages from "El texto devorado" and *Pájaros de la playa* cannot be stressed too strongly, for Wahl notes that when Sarduy had completed the passage in *Pájaros de la playa* he remarked that if only one passage of his work were to remain it should be this one.[*] The remark might seem curious at first, but the more one explores the allusions the passage contains, the more one understands Sarduy's evaluation. Translating the passage enabled us to understand this, because it prompted us to explore not only the multiplicity of allusions contained in the passage but also the several strains or sorts of narrative present in the novel. Wahl refers to these strains as three "strata," each of which required a distinct style of writing (the incidents that involve the patients in the sanatorium, the antics of Immortelle and her physicians, and the Cosmologist's journal).[†]

The passage under discussion here belongs to the first of those layers, since it forms part of a description of the young

---

[*] Wahl, "Severo de la Rue Jacob," p. 1052

[†] *Ibid*.

but aged patients and the challenges presented by such simple acts as getting dressed or taking a short walk. At the same time, however, the presence of the bewildered blonde with the transfusion and the man in the wheelchair allude to the other types of narrative. The lighter, even playful descriptions of the blonde woman and her escape from the sight of the birds suggest the rather jocular sections centered on Immortelle, although Immortelle does not appear in this passage, and the diatribe spoken by the man in the wheel chair links him with the Cosmologist, who, at this point in the novel has not yet resigned himself to his illness nor begun his self-prescribed exercise in non-being. By the time this occurs – in Chapter Thirteen – the man in the wheel chair will have unmistakably become the Cosmologist and his narrative will be designated as such; but in Chapter Two his comments anticipate the Cosmologist's journal, especially since he is clearly identified with the lone bird whose thump on the skylight brings those comments to a close.

One cannot know for certain, of course, precisely what it was about this passage with the birds that particularly pleased Sarduy, but having translated it and considered it in the context of the entire novel and Sarduy's entire production, we would suggest that its value lies in the achievement of a simple, even austere description of the terminally-ill patients that, without altering the nature of that narrative, contains allusions to other texts and incorporates strains (as an actual presence as opposed to an allusion) of two additional, distinct narratives. One of those narratives – which concerns Immortelle – will be quite familiar to Sarduy's readers. The other – that of the not-yet Cosmologist – will not be familiar, since by the end of the novel Sarduy has gradually developed a style unique to this narrator. In particular, as Wahl points out, the final poems in Chapter Twenty-One (supposedly found in a separate notebook) are written in unrhymed, irregular lines that differ markedly from Sarduy's own poems; in addition, the references to San Juan de la Cruz and Christian mysticism contrast with the Eastern ambience predominant in so many of Sarduy's texts.[*]

Through the allusion to Goytisolo's allusive novel, Sarduy's own homage to that novel, and the need to craft unexpectedly – and at a relatively young age – a "late style" reminiscent of the "untimely...last or late period of life" described by Edward Said,[†] Sarduy achieved a style unlike the one that preceded it, one whose rigor would both resemble and differ from his earlier work. Now the rigor would not so much require elaborate constructions opening like infinite Chinese boxes in closed forms as it would demand work with uncertainty, fragmentation, and a new type of non-representation of one's self that would allow Sarduy to describe the painful indignities of illness but at the same time remove himself from that description and acknowledge the impossibility of controlling the end of the tale.

*

As we complete our translation of *Pájaros de la playa*, it is a pleasure to express our thanks to the people who answered our translation-related questions and the institutions that supported our work. In particular, we want to mention the Translation Studies Research Focus Group of the University of California at Santa Barbara's Interdisciplinary Humanities Center for making it possible for Carol to travel to California so that we could produce the final version of the manuscript. In the past our collaborations have been based on the exchange of drafts by us mail or e-mail and long conversations by phone. The opportunity to be in the same room at the same time enabled us to merge our individual drafts and personalities,

---

[*] *Ibid.*

[†] Edward Said, "Timeliness and Lateness," *On Late Style: Music and Literature Against the Grain*, New York: Pantheon, 2006. p. 106

creating a translator who comprises both Jill and Carol – an opportunity we greatly appreciate. To the many friends (and students and faculty at UCSB and UCLA with whom we discussed our translation) who offered helpful responses to our queries about the translation of *Pájaros de la playa* we also extend heartfelt thanks.